PERFECT MELODY

L. A. BURCH

Books by L. A. Burch

The Masterminds Series
Retribution

Beyond Redemption

Reparations

Retaliation (Coming soon)

Standalones
Twisted Reprisals

Perfect Melody

Lyrics Credit: "Ready for love" by India Arie

KDP Publishing

Cover Design: Michelle D. Josey

ISBN: 9798990247253

DEDICATION

Not many people stick by incarcerated individuals. It's super easy to apply the theory of out of sight, out of mind. This book touches on a lot of difficulties in our society, but one that I want to highlight is how much of a difference having outside help can be to someone on the inside. Without it, many just sit around soaking up all the negativity surrounding us on a daily basis. A few minutes here or there with a loved one could ultimately decide whether it's possible for a person to reintegrate back into society. Many who have to make it on their own leave prison bitter and angry for the perceived abandonment.

So, I want to dedicate this book to all the people who keep their locked-away loved ones on their mind. Just remember, a little bit of time given could mean the world to someone who needs just a touch of recognition.

Special Thanks To

Trapp   **J-Boa**

Special thanks to the gentlemen who allowed me
to portray them as thugs in my book.

PERFECT MELODY

Chapter 1

As the two men entered the luxurious apartment, the taller of the two gave a low whistle of appreciation.

"Damn Cousin, you outdid yourself on this one. I mean, the pictures were nice, but this is amazing!" Jeremy Harris continued to gawk at the furnished perfection around him as he dropped his bags on the floor.

"I told you I got you, Jay. Only the best for my little cousin." The look from Jeremy caused him to alter his last statement. "Well, younger cousin, anyway."

Jeremy Harris had the body of an All-Pro wide receiver. At 6-foot 4-inches, 230-pounds, with the muscle definition of someone dedicated to his body, not many people could call him little. Compared to his cousin's 6-foot, 165-pound, slim body, he might as well have been a giant.

Jeremy said, "I know I told you to find something nice with a wide-open floor plan, but I don't know if I can afford this long-term."

"Jay," said Chris Harris. "If this was New York or LA, you still wouldn't have to worry. Remember, you're legally rich now. Anyway, this is Kannapolis, North Carolina. It's only $2,200 a month."

"What!" Jay exclaimed in amazement. "That's it?"

"Yeah, and the first year is paid for already. Not that we had a choice about that," he mumbled under his breath.

"What the hell does that mean?" Jeremy demanded.

"Well, since you wanted the place to be in your name instead of mine, I had to throw in a little incentive to get you approved. I'm sure you realize, not many places like this want to house newly released, convicted felons."

And there it was. Jeremy had to clinch his teeth to hold back a retort. He knew his cousin was right, and no matter how successful he had become, to some, he would always be just a convicted drug dealer.

Chris read the rage in his younger cousin, so he went and sat down on the leather sectional, hoping he would follow. When Jay stood there, looking ready to grab his bags and go, Chris said, "This is a small-town, Jay. They had other places willing to take you, but none compared to this. After being in a box for seven years, I felt that you deserved the best. So, I did what I had to do to get you in here. Come on man, sit down and enjoy your freedom. Don't let these smallminded motherfuckers ruin your homecoming."

Jeremy forced himself to relax, but he didn't take his cousin up on the offer. Instead, he continued walking around, taking a tour of his new home. He got to what he felt should be the master suite, turned the handle, and found the door locked. He turned to Chris, who was sitting in the living room with a huge smile on his face.

"Now Jay, you know me. You know I wasn't gonna let you come home without a little surprise." Chris rubbed his hands together and grinned even wider. "And what a surprise it's gonna be!"

"What the hell, Chris? I told you no surprises or parties. I pray that your surprise is a nice, King-sized bed, and blackout curtains over the windows. I'm tired as hell." Jay could pray all he wanted, but he knew his cousin. He could guess what was on the other side of the door.

Chris jumped up and rushed over, brandishing a key like

it opened the gates to heaven. He inserted the key, turned it, and pushed the door wide open.

Part of Jeremy's prayer was answered. Actually, the whole prayer was answered. There were blackout curtains over the massive windows and sliding glass door that led to the deck. There was also a King-sized bed that was designed to accommodate at least four people comfortably. He came to that conclusion because, he figured he was supposed to make the forth person added to the three naked women sprawled across the bed.

All Jeremy could do was laugh and shake his head at the spectacle in front of him. There was a black one, a white one, and a Latina, all very thick, very beautiful, and because they had started without him, he could assume, very horny.

They looked at him with passion filled eyes and the white woman said, "Sorry, we couldn't wait any longer." She inserted her fingers into the other women and said, "But we're hot and sticky and could really use a big man like you."

Her fingers never stopped moving as fingers entered her and they all three moaned in unison. Jeremy reached out and slammed the door closed. He looked at Chris and laughed out loud. "I love you Chris, and I thank you for all you've done for me. Now, get them hoes out of my bed and out of my home before I beat your ass."

Jeremy started to walk away when Chris asked, "You not even gonna let them finish?" Jay glanced back at him and Chris rushed into the bedroom and started barking orders. "Okay ladies, we're done here. Get ya'll nasty asses dressed and get the fuck out." Jay heard him say a little quieter, "I'll call ya'll later. You know he aint had none in a while, we need to start him on something less intimidating to get him back up to speed."

It only took a minute for all three ladies to exit the bedroom with their slip-on dresses covering just enough to keep them out of jail. As the Latina beauty bent over to put on her stiletto, it was clear to see how they had dressed so fast. None of the women were wearing underwear.

Chris was slapping asses and clapping his hands, trying to get them herded in the direction of the door. Jeremy said, "Sorry ladies, maybe another time."

They waved and blew him kisses but, as Chris opened the door to the hallway, they all pulled up short with shocked faces. Jeremy walked from the kitchen area to see what they were staring at. What he saw caused his stomach to drop.

Standing on the other side of the threshold was a police officer, and she didn't look pleased with what was standing before her.

Chapter 2

Officer Melody Franklin was so close to realizing her dream, she could taste it. Growing up, seeing her dad walk through the door of their Atlanta home in his crisp Atlanta PD uniform, had left a lasting impression on her.

As far back as she could remember, she wanted to be a police officer. Somewhere along the way she decided the work fit her, but the uniform didn't.

So now, six years in, she had her sights set on making detective. Wearing her own clothes and doing police work would make her world complete. Especially after the tragedy of two years ago.

On a typical day in Atlanta, weather hovering around a toasty 80 degrees, sun shining with a slight breeze, her worst nightmare had become reality. Her friend and mentor, Officer Adrian Hampton, had been lecturing her on the intricacies of eating in a squad car. He was describing how to hold your burger and drive at the same time, when a car streamed pass them going well over 100 miles per hour.

They were parked along the backside of a billboard and Adrian immediately hit the lights and gave chase to the speeder. Melody's heart was beating out of control because she expected a prolonged highspeed pursuit. Instead, the driver of the Honda Accord pulled over at the first safe spot they encountered.

Both of them pulled their guns and exited the car, making their way to either side of the Accord. Before they could react, the driver jumped out and pumped a round into Adrian's head. He let off two shots in Melody's direction, causing her to duck down and retreat, giving the man all the time he needed to jump back in his vehicle and speed off.

Melody had called it in, but stayed to render aid to her fallen partner. The worst part was, when the other officers caught up with the suspect, they shot and killed him before anyone could question why he did it. The guy had no warrants, no record, and no contraband in the car. When his toxicology came back clean, everyone assumed he'd had a psychotic episode, shrugged, and closed the case.

Seeing Adrian with all that blood on his uniform, and later seeing it all over her own, had caused her to develop a hatred for the uniform. She had stuck it out another year before she came across an ad looking for officers to come to KPD. They had promised advancement opportunities, so she'd put in her transfer and, for the past year, had been loving the charms of the small North Carolina town.

Pulling up to her apartment building normally signified the end of her day. Today, she had one more task to perform before she could finally turn in.

Melody smiled as she looked at her building, knowing she could never afford to stay in a place like this. It was luxury on a scale she had never been privy to. But, the owners of the housing development wanted a permanent police presence, so she and three other officers got to live in the apartments for free. This caused a little contention in the ranks back at the department, but not enough for any of them to turn it down.

For the last month, Chris Harris had been preparing the apartment next door to hers for his drug dealer cousin to move in upon his release from prison. She had met Chris about a month before he started setting up the home because he needed to convince her to lobby for his cousin's approval to move in. He'd tried to convince her by stating that an officer of her standing would be the perfect person to keep

Jeremy Harris in line. She'd told him she would do a little research and get back to him.

She had looked into his case and found it pretty typical of how most drug dealers were caught. Officers had set up a sting and he had sold a sizeable amount of cocaine to an undercover. He had been 23 years old at the time and painted as a major player in the Central NC drug trade. But, because no drugs, guns, or other type of contraband was found during the raid on his home, he had gotten off easy. No history of crime before the bust led the judge to suspending more than half of his 15-year sentence. After serving seven years, he was now due to come home.

Done researching the case, she had investigated the man. She'd been curious as to how a man fresh out could afford one of the luxury apartments. She'd feared drugs, but after the Google search, she had to admit she was impressed.

Jeremy Harris hadn't wasted his time in prison. Almost from day one he had started writing songs and, using his older cousin, Chris, as his manager, had started selling his songs to some of the hottest R&B and Hip-Hop artist on the planet. He literally had over 100 hits to his credit. As she scrolled down the list, she figured he could buy the whole complex if he wanted to.

Another thing she noticed, but hated herself for, was how fine he was. She didn't really have a type, but if she did, he was it. Big. Chiseled. Clean-shaven. His dark, wave-packed hair just thick enough for a woman to run her fingers through. And that damn smile. She was just looking at one of his prison photos and she was smiling along with him like a dumbass. Melody was nobody's groupie, but she admitted, if he wasn't successful and handsome, she probably would have told the management she would leave if they approved him.

The next day, she had told the owners it was OK with her, and she would also keep an eye out for any illegal activity. Chris had thanked her profusely and started readying the place for the superstar song writer.

Sitting in front of her building now, she looked at the parking spots reserved for apartment 204. There were only four apartments in each building; two on the first floor and two on the second. But, there were 20 building in the gated community.

She lived in 203, so she and her new neighbor would be the only two people with access to the second floor. The apartments were mirror images of each other, so the doors to enter the homes were only about 20 feet apart, despite the vastness of the space. The elevator was smack dab in the middle, so there would be plenty of opportunities for them to run into each other. Then again, depending on their schedules, their paths might only cross every once in a while.

She eyed the familiar all white Range Rover that Chris normally drove, and reasoned that the dark blue one belonged to his cousin, Jeremy. A quick run of the plates confirmed her guess. She huffed out a breath, exited her squad car, and made her way up to the entrance.

Melody only had need of one of her parking spots because, outside of police work, she didn't have a life to speak of. No need to make insurance and car payments on a car she would never use. With Jeremy being so famous, he would probably always have guest over. She made up her mind to not make an issue of it if he needed to use her extra space.

The security was top notch, with cameras and scan cards

at every entrance. She scanned her way into the glassed lobby area, then made her way over to the elevator where she had to scan again to gain access to the second floor. If you didn't have a keycard, you had to be buzzed in at the entrance, then again at the elevator to reach the second floor. Because of Melody and the other officers living in the complex, it was usually calm and quiet with little to no crime. The extra layers of security could be bothersome at times, but you never knew when they would come in handy.

The elevator door opened and she stepped out and glanced longingly at her own door, but ultimately turned to the right to greet her new neighbor. For the past four months the apartment had been vacant, she had started to feel like the whole area was hers alone. She would have to get used to the idea of other people being in what she considered her personal space.

She stopped at the door, and since everything was totally soundproof, she had no idea someone was on the other side as she prepared to knock. Before she had the chance, it was snatched open and Chris stood there, wide-eyed, with three half naked women by his side. Everyone froze and went quiet for a second before she caught movement out of the corner of her eye.

Jeremy Harris, in the flesh, stepped from the kitchen area. What pissed her off the most was that, even with the women's telling presence, speaking to what Jeremy's priority had been upon his release, her heart still jumped in her chest at the sight of his impressive form.

Chapter 3

"What the fuck?" demanded Jeremy. "You better have a warrant for access to this building. If not, I'll have your ass for harassment!" The rage boiled off of him as he stalked towards the door. Everyone scrambled to get out of his way and she even took a couple steps back.

Melody knew he'd never had a violent conviction, but her hand reacted to the possible threat by hovering over her weapon. Seeing this just seemed to make his blood run hotter.

He turned to his cousin and said, "I thought you said this place was secure. If the fucking police can just run up in here whenever they please, that's not what I would call safe."

Now the situation was a little clearer to her. Melody said, "Chris, you didn't tell him?"

Jeremy's head snapped in her direction. "Chris?" He turned back to his cousin with a really intense expression. "You know her? You invited the fucking cops to my home?"

"No, I uh…. It's not, um…." Chris stumbled through his explanation.

Finally, Jeremy backed up and pointed towards the door. He said, "OUT!" and Chris and the three ladies fled to the elevator and disappeared. He then turned to her. "You got that warrant?"

She had been an officer in Atlanta for five years. She refused to be intimidated by the aggressive man. "I don't need a warrant because…"

"Because what?" he cut her off. "Because I'm a felon? Because you're the law and you do whatever you want? I've been home ten minutes and you motherfuckers are already hounding me!"

"Damn! Ten minutes huh? The ladies wore you out that quick?" She knew it was the wrong thing to say as soon as the words left her mouth. Which was confirmed a second later by the door slamming in her face. She thought about knocking so they could hash it out, but thought maybe letting him calm down a bit would be better.

She walked to her own apartment and made a beeline for the bathroom. It was time to wash this day away and hope tomorrow would be better. Even policing in a small town like Kannapolis had its share of bad times. She was in the process of helping a senior detective solve a string of burglaries, and she knew, with his recommendation, the open detective spot would be hers. The hated uniform could finally be taken off for good.

Melody exited the shower, but stopped in front of the mirror where she eyed her naked body. She had never been shy, and she knew she was considered attractive. But now she looked at her body critically, the way a man might.

Her heart shaped face was dominated by huge, hazel eyes and plump, pink, kissable lips. Her crinkly, black hair hung down a few inches pass her shoulders. Her luminous, light-brown skin was without blemish, so she hardly ever wore makeup. At 5-foot 8-inches, she wasn't too tall or too short, she was what one of her past boyfriends called the perfect tucking height. And her 135 pounds made her figure lush and curvy without anything being overtly prominent.

She bracketed her small waist and forced her 36C breast to stand at their proudest. Her dark brown nipples stuck out invitingly, and she had to quickly dispel the vision of a wavy haired, chiseled man leaning down to indulge with his mouth all she had to offer.

Her side and back views were just as enticing. She worked out on the regular, so her stomach was flat and her ass firm, round, and stood up high. She frowned when she thought about the three women who had exited Jeremy's apartment. By no stretch of the imagination was she thick like them. They jiggled in places she wasn't even sure she had. If that was the kind of women he went for, she didn't stand a chance in hell.

Wait! What the hell was she thinking? She didn't want to be with him! He was a convicted felon, for God's sake! She shook her head, hoping to rid herself of her delirium, and went to put on her night clothes.

Even though it was only 8:00pm, she ate a small meal and turned in for the night. Tomorrow was Friday, and she would start work early and stay at it until late. Then she had a couple days off. She would rest and recharge before starting again on Monday.

Normally, Melody's head would hit the pillow and she was instantly asleep after another exhausting day. Tonight, sleep eluded her. Thoughts of Jeremy and his perfect body floated in her mind, keeping her awake. When she would sleep, her dreams were filled with erotic visions of a big, dark-skinned, muscular god, stroking her with precision, making her scream over and over again.

At 6:30am, she woke after another dream, finding her gown pulled up over her waist, her fingers buried deep in her core. The end was so close at hand, she didn't have the power to stop what her unconscious mind had already started. Even half asleep, her fingers played a perfect tune until her climax ripped through her body, leaving her shaken and weak but far from satisfied.

Irritable and achy, she got out of bed and prepared for her day. She had way more important things to think about than her rich and handsome neighbor. Like catching these burglars and taking that pivotal step towards becoming a detective. But even as she left her apartment, she couldn't stop her eyes from cutting to his door. Afraid that they would have another run-in today, but also worried that they wouldn't cross paths at all.

Chapter 4

After a quiet and restful night, Jeremy was up early to go see his parole officer. He dressed casually, in khakis and a button up, then made his way outside. The parole\probation office was part of the Kannapolis Police Department, so he gritted his teeth and tried to prepare himself to mingle with the police, AKA the scum of the earth.

It was a beautiful October day, the sun shining bright and a nice, cool breeze blowing just enough to tease the skin. A smile lit his face as reality hit him. He could come outside whenever he wanted and stay as long as he liked. No lazy ass CO telling him the yard was closed. No bullshit OIC deciding not to open the yard because his fat ass wife didn't give him any last night. Nope, he was now a free man.

The smile dimmed a little when he thought of his parole officer. He had prayed for some old white man who just wanted his piss in a cup and his fees paid. What he got was a young, attractive, curvy, black woman, who he felt would cause him trouble. He would be on parole for the next eight years, and since meeting her while still on the inside, she had been eye fucking him with little discretion. He didn't know if it was his money or his body, but she wanted something, and it wasn't his pee in a cup.

He walked around the dark blue Range Rover and frowned. A thought crossed his mind and he pulled out his IPhone to send a message to his cousin, Chris. By the time he got back home, everything should be taken care of.

Jeremy climbed in and started his 10-minute journey while watching the scenery flow pass. Being born in Charlotte, only a few miles away, he'd been to KP a few times. Mostly, it had been to deliver a pack, or see some chick, but he could clearly see the town was growing.

More businesses and better roads spoke of the town's prosperity. As he pulled up in front of the PD, the downside of that prosperity was on full display. As with any growing city, crime becomes a growing concern, which was reflected in the rows and rows of cop cars.

He parked and made his way into the building, having to show his ID at three different checkpoints before entering the parole office. At each stop, the police eyed him like he was a terrorist, and he wished he could kill them all with his bare hands.

Dirty rotten bastards. The biggest gang in the world and citizens had given them the power to kill us or lock us away whenever they felt like it. Well, fuck that! He hated them more than they hated him, and he didn't try to hide his feelings whenever he encountered one. The difference was, he actually had a reason for his hate.

Jeremy had to calm himself before knocking on Ms. Drye's office door. She waved him inside and said in a seductive voice, "Close the door, honey, so we can have some privacy."

There was no way in hell. He said, "If you don't mind, I'd like to leave it open. I'm more comfortable that way." At her spiteful look, he hurried to say, "You know, after seven years of locked doors, I just hate being in a closed space." She seemed to accept his explanation and motioned him into one of the visitor's chairs.

For the next two hours, that's pretty much how the visit went. She would flirt and send out veiled innuendos, and he would try to shoot them down in a way that wouldn't put him on her bad side. He hated every minute of it, but he made it back out to his vehicle with a minimum of restrictions. He was about to get in when he heard a high-pitched voice calling his name. He turned to see the same female officer from last night.

He waited. Not because he wanted to, but because he was struck by how beautiful she actually was. Last night, the lighting in the hallway had been dim. Now, the sun shined on her natural curly hair and caused her skin to glow with radiance. She reminded him of the Instagram model, Bralynne Hughes. Men on the inside went crazy for the light-eyed beauty.

Even with the uniform on, he could make out her tantalizing curves as she walked towards him. As she got closer, he confessed that she was exactly his type, not those big-bodied women from last night. But the presence of the uniform still soured him on all her high-level attributes.

He moved his arms away from his body and said, "Are you following me? Look, if it will help to ease your mind, get a warrant and then you can search me, my car, and my home. I just want to be left alone."

"I'm not following you, Mr. Harris." She waved her hand to encompass the area. "I work here."

"Alright, so what is it you want from me? I haven't done anything wrong. I paid my debt to society. What? Do you want an autograph?"

"No, that's not…. Well, I wouldn't turn one down but…" She stopped rambling and said, "All I'm trying to tell you is, I'm your neighbor. We share the second floor of Building Two. Last night I was just coming to introduce…"

"Hold on! Hold on! Hold on!" he cut her off. "You live in 203?" At her nod, he barked out a laugh. "Is that how you know Chris?" He allowed his arms to relax by his side, but still didn't make any sudden moves.

"Well, I don't know him, know him," she clarified. "He needed me to put in a recommendation for you to get approved to move in."

"Why would he need your recommendation? I don't understand. Are you on some kind of approval board?"

She shook her head no. "But, those apartments are part of the most exclusive neighborhood in the city. The management just wanted to make sure they weren't putting their residents in danger. I researched you and felt you didn't pose a threat, so they approved you."

Jeremy could feel the anger taking over his mind. "You researched me and deemed me not a threat? Well, fuck your assessment! I didn't ask for your help, and if you think I owe you something, you can think again." He looked at her nameplate. "Now, am I free to go, Officer Franklin?"

Before she could answer, another officer came over with a smile on his face and an outstretched hand. The young black man said, "Hey! You're Jeremy Harris! Can I get your autograph?" The officer pulled his offered hand back and reached in his pocket for a pen and pad. Ignoring the fact that Jeremy was being rude, he kept his smile and extended the items out to him.

Jeremy bared his teeth at the officer and growled, "Fuck you!" before jumping in his Range Rover and pulling off. He was steaming and he placed a call to his cousin to arrange a meet back at the apartment. He wanted to strangle Chris for putting him in this horrific position. He of all people should understand why he couldn't live next door to a fucking cop.

Chapter 5

Damn, thought Melody. She had been so optimistic about this day. Now, it was over and she hadn't accomplished any of the things she'd set out to do.

She and Detective Smalls hadn't found any new leads on the burglaries, and with a new one discovered that very morning, the perps showed no signs of slowing down. The detective assured her that a break was soon to come, but she felt like she was letting him down by not solving the case. Not to mention, her failure was destroying any chance she had at becoming a detective herself.

There was only one Junior Detective spot open and there were five of them vying for the coveted position. She was the only black woman, and she felt she had to do something amazing to set herself apart. So, she had offered her services to one of the senior detectives and he had gladly taken the extra help. He even promised a glowing recommendation if she managed to help him solve the case.

That relaxing weekend off was now only a fantasy. She had copies of all the casefiles in the trunk of the squad car, and she would be using her time off to look for anything they could use to further their case.

She had just turned into Exclusive Oaks, the apartment complex where she lived, when she spotted the blue Range Rover parked alongside the basketball courts. She wished she had the strength to keep her patrol car moving forward, but a sweating, panting Jeremy with his shirt off was an image she couldn't pass up. She pulled in and parked, hoping to get a close-up view.

She didn't see him on the basketball, volleyball, or pickleball courts, so she thought he must be inside at the pool or weight room. Getting ready to put the car back in gear, she took one last glance, and there he was.

Melody wasn't sure this sight was any less dangerous than the first one she'd conjured up. He was sitting at a picnic table reading a book, occasionally glancing up to watch the basketball game in progress.

It was dark out, but the courts were well lit with overhead lights. He was deeply embedded in shadows, but the form she'd been lusting over for the past 24 hours had already become familiar to her. All of a sudden, Jeremy jumped up and took off running towards the courts.

So caught up in her own fantasies, she hadn't noticed the fight going on until after he had taken off. By the time she got there, he had already separated the boys and had everyone laughing at something he was saying.

When he caught sight of her walking up, he raised his hands and stepped back. He said, "Everyone put your hands up and don't make any sudden moves. And don't say a word until your parents get here."

All the kids did what he said until they saw who the officer was. A young black kid dropped his hands and said, "Man, that's Officer Melody. It's cool."

"Hey!" barked Jeremy. "Don't ever trust the cops, okay? Put your hands back up."

The kid waved him off. "Man, you trippin'. Officer Melody is one of the good ones." Turning to dap up a friend, he said, "She fine as hell, too."

Melody fought to keep a straight face as she pointed at the boy. "Jalen, be respectful. And it baffles me how you and John are best friends, but are always fighting. Do I have to go have a talk with your parents?"

"No Ma'am," both boys said in unison.

"Why don't ya'll call it a night, let your tempers cool down, and finish the game tomorrow?"

"Yes Ma'am," they readily agreed, a shimmer of hope that they would get out of the situation without their parents being notified. "Thank you, Officer Melody. See you tomorrow," they yelled as they raced off.

All civility melted off as she spun on Jeremy. "What the hell is your problem? They are only kids, Mr. Harris! You don't tell a bunch of children not to trust the police."

"Why the hell not?" he angrily replied. "Someone has to let them know how dirty you motherfuckers are. I wish someone had told me."

"Look Jeremy, I studied your casefiles. You sold to an undercover cop! He was doing his job. That doesn't make him dirty and it damn sure doesn't mean all cops are dirty. Get over yourself, admit you fucked up, and then move on. Let it go!"

Jeremy was literally shaking with rage. "Don't lecture me on how to live my life. Now, can I go, or am I under arrest?"

Shaking her head in frustration, she said, "Just go, Jeremy." She watched him as he stalked off and jumped in his vehicle, not understanding why he was so hostile towards the police. In a matter of seconds, he was gone, and she slowly made her way back to her own vehicle.

She was so ready for this day to be over. Jeremy was becoming more of a nightmare than the fantasy she constantly imagined him to be. The only thing on her mind as she climbed into her car was a hot shower and a warm bed. Then she saw something fluttering in the wind over by the picnic table.

It was Jeremy's book.

She rolled her eyes up to the heavens as she wondered what she had done to deserve this level of torture.

Chapter 6

A couple hours had passed since the scene at the sports complex and Jeremy was feeling pretty good. He had talked to his mother, who was already asking him when he was coming back for another visit.

He had actually gotten out of prison that past Tuesday. The first two and a half days, he had spent with his mother and various cousins in Charlotte. He'd had a ball, but his family was loud and boisterous, reminding him of the open dorms in the state prisons. They never gave him a moment of peace. He had been extremely happy to make it to Kannapolis Thursday night. His freedom only started to sink in on Friday morning when he had awakened alone in his own home.

More than a little bit had been accomplished during his first full day on his own. He had gotten his probation officer to fall back somewhat. He had cursed his cousin out for setting him up with a cop for a next-door neighbor. But most importantly, Chris had come through with his latest special request.

The Range Rover was good and he'd get a lot of use out of it in the future. But, there was one car he had been dreaming of owning since he was a little boy. It was the dream car that led him down the path of incarceration. This time, though, he didn't have to sell drugs to get it. He could afford to pay for it legally.

Plus, he was a star. He couldn't have two parking spots and only use one. So, he sent his cousin on a mission to find him a Ferrari 812 GTS.

He had found one in Greensboro that could be delivered immediately and, when Chris sent the photos, he had fallen in love with the supercar. That aggressive, road dominating stance was exactly how he remembered it. With its blue and white decor, and roaring engine, it was the best $800,000 he could have spent.

Even though Chris was a huge pain in his ass, he thanked God for him every day. Honest and intensely loyal, Jeremy could trust him in every aspect of his life. Chris could have stolen from him a million times over, but not one cent has ever been misplaced. So, he knew anything his cousin did for him was only to help.

That's why, earlier today, as they had taken the Ferrari out for a spin, he had listened as Chris convinced him to stay in the apartment he was renting. He saw the security and Officer Franklin as the perfect alibi if he ever needed one. Nobody could accuse him of doing something or being somewhere he wasn't if he stuck close to home. Chris reminded him he still had eight years hanging over his head, and it was time to use the police to his advantage instead of antagonizing them at every turn.

After some thought, Jeremy concluded that it made sense. So now, it was 10:00pm on a Friday night, he was a young millionaire, and he was happy and content to sit on his leather couch in underwear, surfing channels on his huge TV.

He had just found a movie he'd been wanting to see when there was a knock on the door. If it was Chris, he would have called and used his key to come right in. So, it only left one other possibility of who it could be.

He was well aware that all he had on was boxer briefs, but he'd be damned if he changed to make her feel more comfortable. She was just starting her second round of knocking when he yanked the door open. And concluded he had made a major tactical error.

You see, Jeremy was young, attractive, famous and rich. Because of those things, a lot of female correctional officers had tried to entice him into their trap. He had never indulged in their games, which led to a long seven years without a woman.

He had known Officer Franklin was good-looking, but he had let the uniform taint her attractiveness. Now, she stood before him barefoot, hair hanging loose, bike shorts emphasizing her well-formed hips and thighs, and a white crop top that showcased her flat stomach. The top also molded to her braless breasts, almost forcing his eyes to focus on their rounded plumpness.

There was no way he could hide his reaction to her beauty, and a faint blush crept from her chest up to her face. She said, "Um, I'm sorry to bother you, but you left your book out at the picnic table. I was gonna wait until tomorrow but then I thought you might want to read before you went to sleep, then you would be up worrying about what had happened to it. So, here it is."

She extended the book out to him but her eyes continued to devour his body. Since he had opened the door, her eyes had only briefly touched his face. Her frank appraisal was having an unwelcomed but significant effect on him. As all he had on was the tight briefs, she could clearly see that the result was growing by the second.

He took the book from her and reached out to lift her chin, tilting her head up so he could meet her eyes. When she looked at him, the thank you he was about to say froze in his throat. The naked lust on her face made him take a step back. Her eyes told him all he had to do was invite her inside and she would fulfill his wildest fantasies. But, no matter how sexy she was, how erotic his thoughts became, he had to remember she was a cop. A good actress who couldn't be trusted.

He cleared his throat when her tongue shot out to wet her luscious lips, trying his best to hide his lower half with the book. He managed to say, "Thank you, Officer Franklin. This is one of my favorite books. I appreciate you bringing it back."

"Melody," the officer whispered, still staring into his eyes.

"Excuse me?"

"Not Officer Franklin, that's my dad. Call me Melody. I mean, we are neighbors, right?"

"Right. Well, Melody, thank you. Uh… have a good night," he said before closing the door. He walked back to the couch in a trance. She had shocked him. Dazed him. What the fuck was he supposed to do now? There was little doubt that his sexy neighbor would be on his mind for the foreseeable future.

He cut the TV off and retired to his bedroom. He picked up the remote to his stereo and turned some R&B on low before he crawled into bed.

The dream he had that night, unsurprisingly, featured a sexy, hazel eyed vixen, wearing bike shorts and a crop top. Her perfect breasts and tight ass being revealed to him after he had the pleasure of stripping the clothing from her body. Once they were both ready, she climbed aboard, prepared to take them both on a ride. Only thing, it wasn't a bike seat her perfect ass was riding on.

Chapter 7

The next week was a slow burning torture that had Melody's fingers busy almost every morning. She couldn't even blame Jeremy because he was going about his life like any other normal person. It was her wicked imagination that was at fault.

After Friday night, when she had spied the huge bulge developing in his briefs, she had become worse than a teenager with raging hormones. Everything she saw that was big, long, and hard caused him and those tight briefs to pop up in her mind. And, if that wasn't torture enough, she snooped on him whenever she could.

Behind their apartment building was a medium sized, manmade lake. Whenever the weather permits, residents go out on paddle boats or row boats to fish or just relax. After seeing some of the boaters out with binoculars, she had decided to install mirror tint on the windows and sliding glass door that faced the lake.

She had felt curtains or shades would limit her view, but the tint would give her the benefit of keeping an unrestricted view without the pervs being able to look into her bedroom. This past week, she had discovered another advantage to the mirror tint. It allowed her the opportunity to become the unseen pervert with a nice, stimulating view.

When Chris had put in the cable workout rig on Jeremy's deck, she had thought nothing of it. But this past Saturday, she had risen early with the intent of taking a few case files out on her deck to review the material. Only, she found out, someone else was putting the early morning, with its nice, spectacular weather, to use.

She stood at the door and watched, feeling like a voyeur,

as muscles flexed and sweat flew, until she was sweating herself. She'd had to take a quick, cold shower before she could move forward with her plan. But, as soon as she came out on her deck, he said, "Good morning," and disappeared inside.

All week, she had gotten up early to watch him workout. She knew it wasn't right, but the lack of romance over the last few years, had her libido working overtime.

Normally, he was out on the deck well before the sun came up, doing Yoga or some form of martial arts before moving onto the cable machine. Every time she came out to join him, he would politely excuse himself, then rush inside.

After the bulge seen around the world, she had no doubt he was attracted to her. It still stung her pride every time he ran off like she was some kind of leper. So, yesterday, she decided to play the girl role and appeal to his healthy masculine pride.

She'd waited until it seemed he was finishing up, then rushed out onto the deck with her sleeping gown on. "Jeremy! I need your help for a minute!"

He turned to her, wiping sweat from his glistening body, and asked, "What's the problem?"

"The pipe under my sink is leaking like crazy and I don't have any tools to even try to fix it. I called management, but they said it would be this afternoon before they could send someone over."

None of this seemed to impress him. "Did you call a plumber?"

"Dammit, Jeremy! I'm just asking for a little neighborly help! I don't want to flood the people under me and cause both of us to have to move out."

His expression said that he thought that wasn't too bad of an outcome, but he eventually relented. "Give me a minute and I'll be right over."

She had already hidden all her tools after loosening the pipe, so she was in the hall waiting when he exited his apartment with his tools.

Jeremy looked around her apartment before stepping in, like he was looking for tripwires or snares set up to trap him. She grabbed his arm and attempted to pull him over to the sink, but he yanked his arm back and said, "Don't touch me," in a low, menacing voice.

She threw her hands up and said, "Fine, I'm sorry. Just trying to lead you to the problem." It only took him about two minutes to fix the pipe and instruct her on the best way to get rid of all the excess water.

When he turned to leave, never once looking at her in the semi-transparent robe, she called his name and asked him to wait. Offers of refreshments or payment were met with negative responses, so she threw caution to the wind and stepped tentatively into the water.

"Why do you hate me so much, Jeremy?" When he kept his head down and his body pointed towards the exit, she walked around in front of him. "I mean, I've been nothing but courteous and kind to you but, from day one, you've been hateful towards me and I don't understand why."

He lifted his head and said, "I don't want any trouble, OK? I just want to live a quiet life and enjoy what I've earned with the people I love."

"Can you stand here, look me in my face, and tell me

that you're not attracted to me? Can you tell me you're not interested in the least?" she asked him.

"I'm not a liar, so no, I can't tell you that. But I'm not looking for a fling or random sex. I'm looking for a woman to spend the rest of my life with. Because of what you are, that can't be you, so there's no reason to go down that path."

"So, because I'm a cop, you can't give us a chance to even be friends?" At his nod, she turned her back on him, feeling more naked than even the transparent clothes should have allowed. When she turned back to him, she felt a fire light in her soul.

"You know what I hear most from convicts?" She didn't wait for him to answer before rolling on. "How they hate to be compared to other convicts. 'Don't group me in with them, I'm not a pervert.' Or 'I'm nothing like them, treat me like an individual.' And I do my best to give everyone that respect. Why can't you give me that same respect and treat me as I treat you?"

She could tell she was touching on one of his raw spots, she just didn't know what else to say to breach his walls. "Melody, I know it's not fair or reasonable, and you won't understand without the benefit of the whole story. As much as I want you, it's just not gonna happen. I'm sorry." He did look sorry, but she wasn't gonna let him off that easy.

"OK. So, in your mind, you can't separate me as a woman and me as a cop. Prove it." At his confused look, she said, "Kiss me with everything you've got, just one time. And if you can still walk out that door, I won't ever bother you again."

Faster than she realized he could move, he grabbed her around the waist and sat her down on the counter top, her legs bracketing his hips lewdly. He moved to within a millimeter of her lips and asked, "One kiss?" At her nod, he closed the distance and fused their mouths together.

The counter was the perfect height for them to feast on each other, but also get the stimulation from other body parts as well. Which became apparent when he grinded his hardening manhood into her core, causing an earth-shattering orgasm to rip through her body. Her toes curled, her legs and arms locked around his body, and she moaned deeply into his mouth. She was ready and willing to take this wherever he wanted to go, just from this tiny bit of contact between their lips and hips.

He held her through her mini-convulsions and then pulled back to stare into her eyes. With barely and inch of space separating them, and with lust shining bright in his gaze, he crushed her. "That was your one kiss. Seems as if you enjoyed it. Can I go now?"

It took everything in her not to smack the shit out of him. Instead, she nodded, moisture glistening on her lips and in her eyes. She never said a word as he picked up his tools and calmly walked out of the door.

Now, it was Sunday morning, and she decided to change up her routine to see if she could regain some of the good feelings she once had for herself.

Chapter 8

"Aw man, I just don't think God would want you driving a Ferrari to church."

"What!" exclaimed Jeremy. "What the hell kind of sense does that make?"

Chris threw his hands in the air. "Now you cussing? Come on man! He gonna kill us before we get there you keep up all this blasphemy."

"Fuck you, Chris! You drag me out of bed to go to church, and now you want to dictate how I act? I thought God said come as you are?"

"He did say that. You're right, Jay. I'm just saying, be a little respectful when it comes to Him, alright. You might not believe, but you wouldn't have all you got without His blessings."

Jay stopped at a red light and glanced at his cousin. "And I wouldn't have spent seven years of my life in prison if it wasn't for Him either."

"Jay, that's over with, you home now. If He wouldn't have intervened you could have ended up doing the whole 15 years. You're young, famous, rich. Stop living in the past or you gonna miss the present and the future. Plus, you do carry some of the blame as far as your prison stay."

"Nigga, I'll pull this car over and beat your ass. You weren't in there. Don't down play seven years of torture, seven years of humiliation, seven years of slavery. If there is a God, nigga, I deserve everything I have. I deserve the money and the cars and the clothes. And I know I wasn't a saint, but fuck you if you think I deserved prison for helping my family."

31

Chris didn't get a chance to respond as the blue lights and the hated, Whoop Whoop, of the police filled the car. Jeremy glanced at his cousin, letting him see in his eyes that he thought this was all his fault.

"Just chill, little cousin. We didn't do anything wrong. Just do whatever they say and let's get out of here." Jeremy knew his cousin was just trying to calm him down, but he wasn't gonna do anything stupid to give the cops a reason to kill them. Not that they needed too much of a reason.

Chris continued to talk as Jeremy found a safe spot to pull the supercar to the side of the road. "Let's just use our best white people voices, act civilized, and we might make it out of this alive."

"White people voice?" asked Jay. "I don't have no white person voice."

"Well, nigga, you better get one fast. Two niggas in a million-dollar car, they about to shoot the shit out of us!"

Jeremy looked over at his cousin and they both burst out laughing. "Chris, you stupid as hell. Thanks man, I needed that."

The two white officers bracketed the car as the one on the driver's side signaled for Jeremy to let his window down. The officer asked, "Sir, are you in a hurry to get somewhere?"

Jeremy tried to dig deep for the white voice inside of him. "No Sir, and I apologize if I was speeding. Me and my cousin here were just on or way to church. You know, we love the Lord!" Chris stickered beside him as Jay tried his best to emulate a middle-aged white guy.

"Is this a Ferrari 812 GTS?" the officer asked him.

"My God, Officer! You sure do know your cars. Just got her about a week ago."

The officer glanced over at his partner and said, "Told you. You're buying lunch." He focused back on Jeremy and a look of recognition touched his face. "Wait a minute! You're that writer. That song writer. Ahhh...... Jeremy Harris!" he said, snapping his fingers.

Jeremy prepared himself to be treated like the ex-convict he was. What came next, there was no preparation for.

The officer's face lit up and he snatched the hat off of his head. "Oh my God!" he exclaimed. "Me and my wife love your music! You've got the Midas Touch: Everything you touch turns to gold. Well, in your case, platinum. Man, if it wouldn't be too much of a bother, could I have your autograph? No wait! How about a picture? With you, me, and the car?"

He and his cousin shared a shocked look before Jeremy climbed out and took several photos with the over-excited officer. He found himself having fun and only begged to leave after he had Facetimed with the man's wife, and Chris said they were running low on time before the service would start.

He hated to admit it, but the cops hadn't been bad at all. From the dopey smile on his cousin's face, he knew Chris wanted to yell 'I told you so.' The rest of the drive to church was uneventful. But one thought was burning in Jay's mind: If he could throw caution to the wind with those officers, and have so much fun, how much more fun could he have with the hot as hell, Officer Melody Franklin.

Chapter 9

Melody thought she was getting to the church early. She thought 10:30am to an 11:00am service would be plenty of time for her to pick a good seat where she could blend in. But the parking lot was jammed packed when she pulled in.

The lot attendant directed her to a reserved area where only official cars could park. It had been a while since she'd been to the predominantly black church, but she did remember they let officers park where they could make a fast exit if necessary.

Before leaving the apartment, she had concluded that it might be a good idea to wear her all-white, dress uniform. It wasn't something she wanted to do, but she wanted a positive presence to be associated with the badge. Plus, if any pictures turned up, it might help that she was representing the department in a positive way.

Melody entered at the back of the sanctuary and stepped to the side to get a better view. Her second and third look confirmed her first one; she didn't know anyone in sight. She took the seat in the far, back right corner and endured both the well wishers and the hostile looks her uniform usually brought. She ignored the looks that were way too lustful for the church environment.

Right at 11:00am, the church fell silent and the choir got to its feet. The back door opened once more and Chris and Jeremy Harris stepped in. Like a set of heat seeking missiles, Jeremy's eyes locked onto her face and he led his cousin to the two empty seats right beside her.

Chris attempted to sit beside her, something she thought would have pleased Jeremy, but he ended up giving Chris a slight push to dislodge him from her side. She knew this wasn't the time or place, but before he could sit down, she had to take a peek at that hot body of his.

Jeremy's suit was custom made, she guessed, by how well it fit. It was so deep a blue you could only tell it wasn't black when the light hit it a certain way. The only jewelry he had on a was blue and white watch that was a name brand she had never heard of, but probably cost more than a new house. Just knowing the little about rich people that she did, she concluded that the expensive watch was brought to match the expensive car he'd just purchased.

As he sat down, he locked eyes with her and leaned close to her face. She thought she would turn into a puddle if he kissed her, but he stopped just short. He smiled and said, "Good morning, Officer Franklin. It's so nice to see you."

He smelled like some kind of exotic plant hidden in the African jungle. It probably contained some type of prehistoric aphrodisiac that caused women to orgasm with one deep breath. She nodded and returned the greeting, trying to convince her heart to calm down.

He was just being nice because they were in church. She reasoned that, if he wanted anything from her, he could have had it the previous morning. So, a smile and a greeting were nothing to get overly excited about. The service started and their focus turned to the front, granting her a slight reprieve when his gaze drifted away from her burning face.

She thought she had a good singing voice, and normally, when she was in church, she let her inhibitions go. Sitting beside this world class, brilliant, musical mind, she couldn't put herself out there to be judged. So, she clapped along as both men proved that they could be on either side of a song and still make money.

Then the preacher started and she felt things get tense with the Harris cousins.

The balding, middle-aged pastor stepped up to the podium with flowing robes and a serious expression. Everyone was silent and still as he looked out over his flock of faithful followers. His eyes seemed to analyze every soul in the room before he decided on the message his people needed.

"What are we here for?" he asked in a quiet, but commanding, voice. When no one said anything, he said, "I'm not getting deep on you already. I'm just asking, why are we inside this building, sitting in these seats, when we could be anywhere else in the world?"

Melody didn't know if he expected a real answer, but he went on after a small silence. "I'll tell you why we're here. We're here because God has a message for each and every one of us. We're here because somebody needs some help. Because somebody is going through something and they think they have to handle it all on their own. Bottom line, we're here to have CHURCH!" he shouted, causing a chorus of "Amen!" and "Hallelujah!" to rain down on him.

The minister blotted his brow with a rag and glared at the mostly silent audience. "I guess ya'll didn't hear what I said. I said," he screamed even louder, "we are here to have CHRUCH!" This time people jumped out of their seats, clapping and praising God with enthusiasm. The pastor soaked up the noise that only seemed to hype him up more.

He walked from behind the podium and continued down the steps of the pulpit. "Now, my message today might piss some people off," he said, causing everyone to sit down and focus on him again. "This might be the last time I see some of ya'll. But you know what? I. Don't. Care!" he screamed, shouts of "Preach" and "Amen" followed his proclamation.

"God gave me this message and somebody in here needs to hear it. So, if at any time, I get under your skin, or I offend you in any way, I welcome you to use the back door or either one on the sides. Because SATAN! You will not stop this Word from getting out!"

The old, black man at the organ played a few notes and the congregation surged to its collective feet, offering up praises with raised hands. While his flock went crazy, the pastor walked to a small table and took a sip of water before blotting his brow and mouth. He let the praise go on for a while and then used his commanding voice to bring the attention back to him.

"My Brothers and Sisters in Christ. I want to touch on a saying that we've been hearing all our lives, but might not fully understand: God don't come when you want Him, but He's always on time. Can I get an Amen?"

"Amen!" "Praise God!"

"A lot of people don't really understand the full scope of that message. See, they have this vision of God showing up with a fist full of cash when they broke. Or showing up with a key to open that locked door. But, just because you scream, 'Help me God' don't mean He's coming with the help you expect. Can I get a witness?"

"Preach it!" "Hallelujah!"

"But our God!" he shouted with raised hands. "I said, but our God, Uh! He aint gonna let you off that easy, Uh! You see, sometimes, Uh! we think we done got away with some stuff, Uh! We feel like God done forgot, Uh! what we did back in the day, Uh! But, how many of you know, Uh! that God don't forget, Uh! My God, my God, can I get an

Amen?"

"Amen!"

The organ player was now punctuating every one of his sentences with a little ditty that seemed to just flow with his words. Melody looked around as people danced in the aisles and cried out praises to God. Both Jeremy and Chris were on their feet, but they just looked dazed from the message. The preacher went on, whipping the crowd into a frenzy.

"So, when we get punished, Uh! for something we think we're innocent of, Uh! we holler to the heavens 'But God, why me?' Uh! 'But God, I'm innocent.' Uh! But how many of you know, Uh! that it aint God who don't understand, Uh! It's not God who done forgot, Uh! It's all that stuff you thought you got away with, Uh! and He's finally callin' in that debt, Uh! GLORY," he shouted, looking up to the heavens. "Give God some praise," he commanded, turning the sanctuary into a madhouse of worship.

For the next five minutes, it was controlled chaos. Three young church ladies jumped up and started fanning the minister. Three other women had to form a daisy chain around an older lady who was dancing, filled with the spirit. People were shouting, and dancing, and running up and down the aisles.

The choir stood up and the organ came alive with a fast, foot stomping beat. The choir just kept clapping and yelling, "Rejoice. Rejoice. Rejoice." to the beat of the drums that joined the organ. Everybody's dancing seemed to take on the rhythm of the song being played, and everyone's movements started to sync up.

Melody was so caught up in the sights and sounds that it took her a minute to realize something was going on at the front of the church. By the time she noticed, everyone was standing up, craning their necks and blocking her view. Then, an eerie silence fell over the whole building.

She could see the pastor back up on the pulpit and the choir standing at attention. But, whatever it was that held everyone's gaze, was lost to her. Then, she heard it.

"Ahhh haaa know Ah've been changed." The haunted voice seemed to send a chill through the whole congregation.

"Ah said dat Ahhh haaa know Ah've been changed." There was no music playing, but the swaying footfalls of the people sent up a *Thump! Thump! Thump!* beat that was all the song needed.

"Good Lord say Ahhh haaa know Ah've been changed." Like the whole church was on one accord, everyone sang, *"You know the Angels in heaven done signed my name."*

Jeremy finally noticed her trying desperately to see the front, and he motioned for her to remove her shoes and stand on the pew. She did as she was instructed and was greeted with a sight straight out of a B.E.T. movie.

A wizened black woman with flowing silver hair was sitting in a wheelchair with her eyes closed and tears streaking down her face. Two young men, who had to be brothers they looked so much alike, were on either side of her as her voice continued to move the masses.

"Ah stepped in da wahda and da wahda was cold." The church added, *"You know the Angels in heaven done signed my name."*

"It chilled mah body butttt not mah soul." *"You know the Angels in heaven done signed my name."*

Then the whole church sang, as one of the men wheeled

the old lady back to the front row. *"I know I've been changed. I said I know I've been changed. I know I've been changed. You know the Angels in heaven done signed my name."*

Like a choreographed show, everyone sat down except for the choir, who continued to hum as the pastor took over once again. "Thank you, Sista Joyce. That was truly amazing." He blotted his face before he leaned on the podium to address the church. "How many people out there know that fire purifies?"

He was speaking quietly now. It was easy to tell that he was now delivering the message he had come to give. "See, while we sitting back complaining, claiming how unfair God is treating us, and how unfair life is, we can't see the plan that God has. Cause he could have left you out there to get shot. To get stabbed. To let the hooks of the devil sink in so deep, your soul would be lost forever.

"Ohhh, but not the God I serve. Somebody look at your neighbor and say, 'Not my God.'" When the words of the congregation died down, he said, "My God showed you mercy. My God showed you love. But he decided to dangle your feet over that purifying fire for a bit. Let some of that life changing heat seep into ya bones. Can I get an Amen?"

"Amen!" "You better preach!"

"And he does that so, when you're back on solid ground, you remember where you been. What you been through. And, when you get a glimpse of the whole picture, a picture that God saw before the beginning of time, you'll understand why God didn't come when you wanted Him, but He was definitely right on time. Can I get an Amen?"

"Amen!" echoed the congregation once again.

Melody sat and soaked up the lesson. Jewel after jewel as the minister seemed to touch on what each person was going through. By the end, more than a couple people had tears rolling down their face. She was praying that one of the lessons was enough to get Jeremy to put his hatred of the police behind him.

Jeremy and Chris went to talk to the preacher after the service and she stood outside waiting for them to emerge. Half of the congregation was gathered around something at the back of the parking lot. Without seeing what it was, she guessed it was Jeremy's Ferrari. Why people spent so much on something to get them from point A to point B was baffling to her.

"Oh no," she said as Jeremy stepped out of the door at the same time the cop car drove up, dispersing the crowd.

Not knowing what was going on, Jeremy and Chris took off running towards the parked car. Melody went the other way and got her squad car before circling around from the backside of the church. Things had escalated fast, as she saw both officers with hands on their weapons, barking orders.

She jumped out to shouts of, "Get on the ground, now!" and "Keep your hands where I can see them." Chris was on the ground, but Jeremy kept asking, "Why? No! Tell me why!"

When both guns came out, she stepped up. "Hey! What's the problem here?"

Both cops were black men. The older one said, "We got one that don't want to listen."

"Why are you putting him on the ground? We just left church. What did he do?"

"We got a report that drugs were being sold out of that car. We were about to take a look when the big guy came up talking trash and acting aggressive. All we want is him on the ground so we can de-escalate the situation."

She looked at Jeremy's face and knew that no amount of force, short of a bullet, would make him lay down. She also looked at the officers and knew they wouldn't allow the loss of face in front of so many witnesses. In order to save his life, she had to back the officers.

"Jeremy, please just lay down. I won't let anything happen to you, but I can't help you unless you follow their orders."

"I'm not asking for your help. I don't need anyone's help," Jeremy proclaimed.

The two officers pointed their weapons at him. "This is your last warning," the older man shouted. "Lay on the ground or I will put you down!"

Chris pleaded. The crowd pleaded. Melody pleaded. But she didn't plead with Jeremy, she pleaded with God. Pleaded with Him to spare the life of the man He had put so much work into. So much love into.

Like he was coming out of a trance, Jeremy glanced at the crowd, then at Chris, and finally locked eyes with Melody. With tears streaming down her face, she silently pleaded for him to live.

In his expensive suit, with his expensive watch on his wrist, next to his expensive car, Melody saw the young, scared boy he'd once been in life, flash across his face. She saw the hurt, the humiliation, and the pain reflected clearly in his eyes as he fought his pride, which was telling him to die rather than submit.

One tear tracked down his face before he kneeled down in front of his oppressors, who looked just like him. And her heart broke because she knew he would have died right then and there if God hadn't answered her plea, right on time.

Chapter 10

Almost a month had past since the incident at the church, but Jeremy was still a little gun shy about going out in public. He had promised the minister he would become a regular attendee to his Sunday service, but now Jeremy took an UBER instead of driving one of his expensive vehicles. He was a man of his word, so he showed up every Sunday, but he wasn't about to risk his sanity or his freedom with another run-in with the police.

So, writing and working out had become his solace. He figured, if it worked while he was in prison, it had to work in the real world. He had even started selling his songs to new, up and coming artist, something he hadn't done since the beginning of his career. Not because he started drinking his own Kool-Aid, but because most new artist couldn't afford his rising prices.

He had now developed a system of co-writing with the newer artist so that they could off-set the majority of the cost. He gave back to his community on many different levels, but this way was near and dear to his heart. He felt if he'd had a positive influence in his life early on, then he would have made better decisions in his youth.

Jeremy was at his computer, working on a song with a 17-year-old phenom the Tuesday before Thanksgiving, when there was a knock on his door. It could really only be one person, but since the incident, they'd only had one brief encounter.

A week after he had been forced to lay on the ground, Chris came into his apartment with Officer Franklin trailing behind him. She had very formally told him that the two officers had been suspended for their actions and she'd been sent to deliver an unofficial apology from the department.

She had searched his face, he guessed looking for some form of forgiveness, but he really didn't have any to offer her. After her speech, he had ushered them both out the door and returned to his workout. They hadn't spoken since, even though they saw each other at church every Sunday. So, he was curious as to why she was at his door. He closed down the session with the promising young artist, closed his office door, then made his way to the front door.

Jeremy opened his door to the sight of a stunning woman, and a pretty, young girl, both of whom bore an uncanny resemblance to Melody. Before he could open his mouth, he was being hugged by the very attractive lady.

With her arms around him, she said into his chest, "Sorry, sorry. I just had to hug you. I feel like I've known you all my life." She finally let him go and stepped back next to what had to be her daughter, before she made introductions.

"Hi, Mr. Harris. My name is Harmony Nash, but you can call me Mony. And this here is my lovely daughter, Jazmine, or Jazzy, Nash. Melody, my sister, told us to leave you alone, but she's at work and I had to come over and meet you."

Jeremy studied the mother and daughter combination and couldn't help but smile and invite them in. Once inside, Mony said, "Wow! Did you decorate this yourself?" They were both trying to respect his privacy, but necks were stretching to pick up every detail in sight.

"No," he answered. "And I didn't even question who did. When I got out, my cousin handed me the keys, and I made it my home." If they knew who he was, they already knew he'd been in prison. So, he didn't see any reason to try and skirt the issue.

"Well, I'm just glad you're doing so well. I imagine the transition is a lot easier when you have something to come home to," Mony said.

"I don't know about easier, but I suspect a little less worrisome," he answered truthfully.

She snatched her daughter back to her side and said, "Here we are, invading your home. I'm so sorry. I did have a reason for coming over, besides just wanting to meet you."

As she appeared to be gathering her thoughts, he studied the combo closer. Mony had the same exact body type as Melody, but having a child had softened her curves somewhat. At first glance, Melody and Harmony could be twins. But, after a closer inspection, you could see that Mony was a tad bit older.

With lighter eyes, and straighter hair than her younger sister, she was still super sexy, and would turn male and female heads wherever she went. Even with the business attire covering her body, there was no hiding the fact that Harmony was built for pleasure.

Jazmine had been quiet, except for a subdued hello when her mom had introduced her. But he could clearly see an intelligence and curiosity that shined bright through her luminous eyes. She would break a lot of hearts when she was older. There was little doubt that she would develop to look just like her mom and aunt.

She was wearing teenage vacation gear: Jeans, sneakers, hoodie. Something told him she wasn't normally this quiet and shy. Her mother kept sending her concerned looks like she was trying to figure out why her daughter was acting so strange. In the end, Jazzy wandered off, looking at his things, while her mother got to the real reason for the visit.

"Well, like I said earlier, my little sister ordered me to leave you alone. But, it seems that she and your cousin, Chris, had a conversation about you. She was told that you weren't going home for Thanksgiving." Every few seconds, her eyes would track to her daughter. He gestured that Jazzy was fine, so she continued on with her thought.

"So, basically, me and Jazzy came up here from Atlanta to be with Melody because she couldn't get away from work. And, I wanted to invite you to spend your Thanksgiving with us."

Jeremy let the offer float in the air for a second before asking, "Did you talk this over with Melody?"

She chuckled sexily and said, "Your Boo seems to think that you hate her because she's a cop, and you'd rather spend Thanksgiving back in prison than spend it with her. Now, she has to be wrong about that, right?"

Jeremy was confused. "My Boo?"

Her smile lit the room. "Your cousin is very entertaining. He told Melody how you were secretly in love with her and, if she quit the force, you would ask for her hand the next day. But to answer your question, no, I didn't talk it over with her. I didn't want her to be hurt if you said no."

This woman was so real he felt he couldn't lie to her. "Truth is, I'm very attracted to Melody." She started to smile, but he held up his hand to signify more to come. "But, her being a cop is a deal breaker for me. I have a complicated history that makes cops sickening to me."

Harmony nodded her head in thought before

responding. "Chris told her about the two cops you encountered before going to church that Sunday. He thought that you had reached a milestone with your problem. He said it was the happiest he'd seen you since before you turned 15 years old. Now, I don't know you, and I won't pretend to be wise on fixing personal biases. But, if you don't mind, can I give you some advice?"

Jeremy wanted so badly to tell her that he, in fact, did mind, but something about this woman spoke directly to his soul. Her innate goodness pulsated off of her in waves. He said, with a smile, "I would never turn down good, sound advice."

She made sure to capture his eyes before she spoke. "Jeremy, I think you are a beautiful man with a beautiful soul, and it comes through very clearly in your music. But, emotions that can become all-consuming, such as hate, can start to permeate every aspect of a person's life.

"When my husband left me with a 2-year-old girl to raise on my own, I developed a deep hatred for all men. Over time, I started to see that my hatred was hurting the thing that I loved most in the world: My daughter.

"So, instead of letting the hate for some bastard that didn't even matter anymore consume my life, I let the love of my family fill me up from the inside out. My advice to you, don't keep embracing and feeding your hatred. Give another, more powerful, emotion a chance to blanket your heart."

She was too much. The situation was too much. Jeremy found himself wiping away tears he hadn't even known had fallen. Mony stepped to him and wrapped him in her comfort. He couldn't say how long they stood there, but when he finally pulled away, she still had the same beautiful smile on her face, and her own eyes were bright with unshed tears.

He cleared his throat and said, "Your husband was a coward and a fool."

She smiled even brighter and said, "I know."

Jeremy looked around for Jazzy and found her watching them with a grin splitting her face. She said, "Do you realize how many followers I'll get if you become my uncle? I would rule my high school."

The tension evaporated and all three of them burst out laughing.

Once calmed, Jeremy said, "Thank you, Harmony and Jazmine. Thank you for this and the invitation. I would have loved to spend Thanksgiving with ya'll, unfortunately I do have a prior engagement. But, anytime ya'll want to hang out before you return home, just let me know."

They all exchanged numbers and Jeremy led them over to the door. For the second time in as many months, when he opened the door, a not too pleased Melody was standing on the other side. This time, she looked at all of them, frowned, and just walked away without a word or backwards glance.

Chapter 11

Thanksgiving Day and Melody was stuck behind the wheel of an unmarked police car. It was a mild day, gray clouds floating across the sky making the 50-degree day look as if it should be snowing. The inside of the vehicle was toasty and warm, but temperature was the farthest thing from Melody's mind.

Actually, what should have been on her mind was the farthest thing from it. She was supposed to be using the unmarked to set up surveillance on some guys suspected of the burglaries. Until a week ago, that's what she'd been doing. Then, she started noticing Jeremy leaving early every morning and it peaked her curiosity.

He was never dressed for working out, or for a meeting. He would be casually dressed and something about his movements spoke to her suspicious nature.

Her biggest fear was finding out he was back selling drugs, but she had a sneaky feeling that whatever he was up to would involve some woman. She envisioned some bright eyed, big booty chick convincing Jeremy to get back in the game. Or maybe he had just found a woman who appealed to him and he didn't want anyone to know. Whatever the case may be, she made up her mind to find out what it is.

So far, every morning, he'd been going to a warehouse in the next city over, staying for a few hours before heading to the YMCA back in Kannapolis. This morning, he broke routine and headed straight for the 'Y', which boasted a sign saying it would close at 10:00am. A glance at her dash showed that the place had been closed for 45 minutes, but he was still on the inside.

Movement at a side door caught her attention. And there

it was. She had convinced herself that him being a drug dealer was her biggest fear, but she could have handled that. The sight of the bright eyed, big booty, light-skinned bitch with her long, flowing hair, looking up into Jeremy's face with awe, would have brought her to her knees, if she wasn't already sitting down.

She watched them for a bit as they talked, then the woman locked him into a tight embrace, kissed his cheek, hurried over to his Range Rover, and drove away. Melody was aware of Jeremy watching the woman until she was out of sight and then stepping back inside the YMCA.

Melody hammered the steering wheel a few times in frustration before starting the car and pulling off. She'd followed the man for a week so she could get answers, now she had them. While she'd been sitting out in cars, worrying and praying for his safety, he'd been laying up with some donkey-butt bitch. Well, fuck him! If he couldn't see beyond her uniform then she'd start treating him like the criminal scum he was.

She drove around doing her rounds until the end of her shift. After she turned in the unmarked for her regular patrol car, she found herself heading back towards the YMCA. The lovers were probably at the woman's house by now, but to Melody, that building was the scene of the crime.

When the YMCA came into view, she was greeted with a sight that didn't make sense to her. The parking lot was packed with cars, and there were even a couple school buses parked along the side of the building. And, closer to the back sat one of the tractor-trailers she'd spied outside that warehouse in Salisbury.

Her senses told her to drive pass because, now she was positive something nefarious was going on. She wondered if this was the drug ring he'd been a part of and they thought they were safe to meet because it was Thanksgiving night. Even for drug dealing scum, it was pretty low to use a YMCA on Thanksgiving for a meet. She wanted to call in for backup but decided she needed to be sure before she ruined everyone's holiday.

Since it was dark out and most people were indoors celebrating, she just pulled over on a side street and changed out of her uniform top in the car. She left on the pants and added a black turtle neck and her department issued police jacket. This way, she could blend in a little, but also announce herself as police with the Logos on the coat.

She switched out her boots for black sneakers, in case she had to run from the scene, and jogged back to the 'Y' to start peeking in windows. Since most of the walls were floor to ceiling glass, she had to be careful and stay in the shadows to avoid becoming a target. She decided to check out the parking lot after seeing nothing of merit in the windows.

The front row confirmed that some major players were in attendance. There were three Bentleys, two Rolls-Royces, a Bugatti, and a couple Lamborghinis. Not to mention a fleet of BMWs, Benz's, and Range Rovers, of which Jeremy's was front and center. With this many big wigs at the same meeting, there was bound to be a slew of security and sentries. But, as she looked around, none were in sight.

Melody bobbed and weaved her way through the shadows until she reached the dark receiving area of the building. She reached up and pulled, surprised to find the door unlocked. She slipped in and plastered herself to the wall as she let her eyes adjust to the darkness.

She heard the voice of a female around the corner and down the hall, so she drew her weapon and held it along her leg, all the while, preparing her mind for anything. Quietly, she progressed towards the voice and tried to pick up on what she was saying.

Horrible luck, as soon as Melody got close enough to tell the woman was on the phone, she heard her say she had to go because someone was coming. Still not able to see the woman, Melody wasn't sure if she was the person the woman heard coming. She got her answer about five seconds later.

A man with a deep voice opened a door to the left and asked, "Chanel? Are you alright?"

The voice of the woman said, "Yeah Peanut, I'm good. Can I help you with something?"

"Just wanted to make sure you had enough to eat. You know the little soldiers are gonna clean the tables before long."

She laughed and said, "Let them eat. You know they probably never had food like this." She paused and said, "Jeremy is a beast for putting all this together. I didn't know so many shot callers owed him so much."

"Yeah," the man replied. "He put a lot of work in while he was on the inside. Now, when he calls, we really don't have a choice but to come. Listen, I have to get back. If you need anything, hit any of us on our cells and we're on the way."

"Thank you so much," she said with emotion. "You guys really are Rockstars."

With that, the man went back into the main YMCA recreation area and the woman went quiet.

It was really only a formality at this point. After all the

talk of shot-callers and soldiers and work being put in on the inside, there was no doubt that this was what she thought it was. But Melody still wanted to be sure. She slowly made her way to the edge of the corner and checked the doorway to the left. It was clear. So, she lifted her gun to chest level and turned the corner to confront the woman, Chanel.

Lo and behold, it was the bight-eyed, big booty, light-skinned bitch with the long, flowing hair. Her eyes grew wide as Melody approached with the gun pointed directly at her center mass.

Melody quietly said, "Back up from the counter and let me see your hands." The woman obeyed without objection, but with fear clearly on her face. Melody kept the gun trained on the woman as she rounded the counter and joined her on the other side.

She gestured with the gun for the woman to go into the office area and Chanel backed up through the doorway with Melody following. Once inside, Melody closed the door behind them and breathed a sigh of relief now that she wasn't so out in the open.

Just to see if the woman would lie, Melody asked, "What's your name?"

In a trembling voice, she answered, "Chanel Stevens."

"And what are you doing here, Ms. Stevens?"

She glanced around in confusion before saying, "I work here."

Melody laughed. "I've been coming in here for a year now and I've never seen you. Don't lie to me again."

Crying softly, Chanel said, "I just got hired last week. I swear I'm not lying to you!"

"If you work here, why is the receiving area so dark?" asked Melody.

"The YMCA gave us permission to use the rec area for the event, but fire code said we couldn't lock the doors with so many people inside," Chanel explained. "So, management told us to keep everything dark to discourage people from walking in."

"And just what the hell is this event?" asked Melody.

"Chanel?" yelled a voice from the other side of the door. "Sweetie, are you alright in there? Open the door." The knob jiggled and Melody was glad she'd had the foresight to lock it when she closed it.

"Chanel! Say something or I'm gonna knock the door down!" Now that her heart had slowed a bit after being jolted by the surprise interruption, she could hear the voice a little better. Jeremy was on the other side of the door.

Melody motioned for Chanel to lay on the floor and she cuffed her hands behind her back. There was no need for her to catch a bullet if she was just a dishonest employee.

Jeremy was now ramming his shoulder into the door and screaming Chanel's name. The door splintered, then cracked, and finally burst open and hit the wall.

"Girl, what the hell…?" Jeremy started, stopping when he saw Melody holding the gun. "Melody?" he asked as he spied Chanel handcuffed on the floor. "What the fuck are you doing here? And what did you do to Chanel?"

"What I'm doing here is locking up a bunch of drug dealers. And what I did to her is the same thing I'm about to do to you. Now, turn around and put your hands behind your back," she demanded.

Jeremy paused for so long, Melody started to wonder if she could shoot him if she had to. Then, he smiled, gave a little shrug, and turned around with his hands linked behind his back.

She approached warily, but got the cuffs on without incident. She spun him around, ignored his amused expression, and pushed him farther into the room to keep him from escaping. With no more sets of cuffs, she had no choice but to call it in before she faced the rest of the crew.

She had just pulled out her radio to place the call, when a furious voice behind her said, "Officer Franklin? What the hell are you doing?" She knew then that she had gotten everything wrong. Furthermore, she'd be lucky to have her job at the end of the night.

Chapter 12

The Commissioner of the KPD said, "Once again Mr. Harris, I'd like to offer my most sincere apology. And I can guarantee that this insult won't go unpunished."

Jeremy looked at Commissioner Daniels and then glanced at Melody, who was standing about ten feet away, looking totally dejected. Finally, he said, "Commissioner, Thanksgiving shouldn't be a time when we're dishing out punishments. I'll accept your apology, but only if you promise to let this go and don't hold it against Officer Franklin."

The man looked surprised. "Are you sure? Because if I were you, I'd be pissed right now. She ruined the event!"

Jeremy smiled and said, "Yes Sir, I'm sure." He glanced again at Melody, who was now staring at him in confusion. "She's a good cop who was just doing her job. If we had more officers like her on the streets, this country wouldn't be so divided right now."

The Comish extended his hand and, after they shook, he walked over and whispered something to Melody. She nodded and cast her eyes in his direction before dropping her head and making her way over.

Jeremy greeted her with a deep belly laugh. When he was under control, he said, "A drug dealer's convention on Thanksgiving? Inside of a YMCA? You really do think I'm the scum of the earth."

"Jeremy, I'm..." she began.

"No, no, no!" he interrupted. "I think I deserve to talk a little bit before you bat those beautiful eyes and toss your gorgeous hair around and offer up your most sincere apology," he said, mocking the Commissioner. Angry color rose to her face, but she nodded and gestured for him to continue.

"I've known you were following me all week," he stated calmly. "See, one of the things I learned when I was dealing was to always be paranoid. Seven years in prison just strengthened it. I saw that, the first two days, you had your regular squad car. Then you switched it for the unmarked. You proceeded to follow me all over, and I couldn't understand why. None of the places I went were suspicious, so it took me a while to conclude you thought I was back selling drugs. I figured you would bust in on one of the places eventually, and learn the truth. How do you feel now?"

They were standing in front of the YMCA, watching the Hip-Hop and R&B talent laugh and joke around before leaving one by one in their luxury vehicles. The kids from the low-income neighborhoods in Kannapolis had already been loaded on the buses and shipped out following the Thanksgiving concert and free food. The city council and other elected officials had all left to spend the rest of the holiday with their families. Out of the 200 people who had been invited to the charity event put on by Jeremy, only the clean up crew and YMCA faculty remained inside.

Melody looked deep into his eyes with tears threatening to spill down her cheeks. She said, "I am so sorry, Jeremy. With all my heart, I'm sorry. I shouldn't have judged you and I should have showed a little more faith in your rehabilitation. I can only pray that one day you can find it in your heart to forgive me."

Melody was one of those women who looked beautiful when they cried. He felt his heart soften as he pulled her to his side and said, "We're good, Melody. But you might want to apologize to Chanel though."

She wiped her face and gave him the 'You must be crazy' look before he laughed and explained. "She ended up doing a couple years behind bars for being loyal to her man, who turned out not to be loyal to her. He lied and said the drugs the police found in their car belonged to her. Since the car was registered in her name, she was convicted. Everyone knew the drugs really belonged to the boyfriend, so the judge showed mercy and reduced her ten-year mandatory sentence down to two. No one in the prosecutor's office objected.

"I sort of knew her before I got locked up, we have a lot of mutual friends. When I got out, I was told she wasn't doing too well. I got her into drug treatment and pulled some strings to get her this job. Before I sent her home, all she kept asking was if I thought she would be fired. You really did scare the shit out of her."

Without realizing it, they found themselves walking along one of the dark paths, with her tucked under his arm. For a while, they were both quiet, just walking along. Then Melody asked, "Why are you being so nice to me? And why did you help me keep my job? I thought you would be thrilled to have one less cop to worry about."

Jeremy let a full minute pass before he lowered his arm from her shoulder and stopped walking to answer her. "I didn't lie when I said you were good at your job. I don't have to like a person to recognize they're good at what they do. Take Kevin Durant for instance. I hate that coward ass, skinny fuck. But I recognize his greatness when it comes to basketball. Even if he had to steal the two rings he 'earned.'

"Anyway, I helped you keep your job because there isn't a doubt in my mind that, once you found out you were wrong, you would have done everything in your power to correct your mistake. That's what makes people good, in my opinion. Not that you never make mistakes, but when you do, you own up to them and do whatever it takes to make it right."

It wasn't very cold out but neither of them wore thick jackets. They found themselves drifting closer to share their body heat, at least that was the excuse he told himself. She asked, "And the other part? Why are you being so nice?"

"Well, to be honest, I'm hoping you'll put in a good word for me with your sister." She gasped and pulled back from him. She saw the teasing look on his face and she punched him on the arm and called him a few choice names.

After they both stopped laughing, he said, "Really, it was your sister. When she came over with Jazzy to invite me to Thanksgiving with ya'll, she gave me some really good advice. I won't go into detail, but your sister is a very wise and strong woman. I felt like she was sent to me because I needed to hear what she had to say."

"So, what are you saying, Mr. Harris?" Melody asked huskily.

He leaned down and brushed his lips on her forehead and said, "Go home and be with your family, Officer Franklin. I'll see you tomorrow."

She took a deep breath and slowly released it while momentarily closing her eyes. She looked up at him and said, "You sure?" At his nod, she took a step back and shrugged. "Your loss," she said as she turned to head back up the path, putting a little more sway in her hips than usual.

He watched her until she was out of sight and then brushed a hand down his face. Jeremy was not gonna hurt that woman. He was gonna make damn sure his bias was completely gone before he put his hands on her. He vowed to take things slow and build a friendship before they took it any farther. He prayed that God would give him patience because, if she swung her perfect ass in his face like that again, he would be forced to see if Officer Melody Franklin tastes as good as she looks.

Chapter 13

Later that night, Jeremy found himself lounging at home, exhausted and hungry. There was no way he would have deprived those kids of a drop of food, so he hadn't eaten anything all night. Now, he was so tired, all he could do was sit on his couch and curse his grumbling stomach.

The knock on his door had him glancing at his watch to see just how late it was: 1:00am. Seeing as he hadn't buzzed anyone up, it had to be Melody. He groaned because he didn't think he could resist her twice in one night, but he still got up and walked to the door.

When he opened it, the first thing he saw was the huge helping of food on the plate. Then it registered who was holding up the plate.

"Uh, hey Jazzy. What are you doing up so late?"

"Heard you had a rough night and thought you could use some leftovers."

He stepped out and glanced down the hallway. "Does your mom and aunt know you're here?"

"Why?" she asked, cocking her head. "You plan on abducting me and holding me for ransom?" She asked it so seriously that he barked out a laugh.

"So, this is the Jazmine your mother was looking for the other night," he stated, stepping back into the apartment. "Come on in, and it's nice to finally meet you."

"Ha-ha! Very funny," she remarked, handing him the plate and following him in.

"While I'm heating this food up, you want to tell me

why you snuck over here under the guise of bringing it?"

"Well, me and my mom are leaving on Sunday, and I needed to ask your opinion on something that's very important to me."

He removed the food from the microwave, took a seat at the island, and then said, "Shoot," before tucking into the food.

"I need you to be brutally honest with me because I'm a big girl and I can handle the truth, okay?"

The food was delicious and he was having a hard time concentrating on anything she was saying. "Yeah, sure. Honest and truthful is my middle name."

She waited a beat until he looked up at her, then she said, "I want to be a singer." He almost unloaded a joke, but he saw that she was intensely serious about this.

"Jazzy, I write songs. I'm not really a talent scout. Now, if you're serious, I can call some people tomorrow…" She was already shaking her head.

"I don't have the confidence for that yet. I've been told by people I know that I'm pretty good. But, before I make a fool of myself, I need someone who has heard real talent tell me if I'm talented enough."

No matter how good the food was, this young lady was coming to him for help. He pushed the plate away so he could give her the respect and honesty she deserved. He said, "Alright, but I'm going to be honest with you. I'll tell it exactly as I see it and hear it. And, I get to pick the song. Okay?"

She thought on it for a bit and then nodded. He asked, "Do you know *Ready for Love* by India Arie?"

She smiled and said, "Sure. It's actually my mom's favorite song."

He leaned back in his chair and said, "Let's hear it."

She walked over and stopped about ten feet from him, took a few deep breaths, closed her eyes, and started to sing.

"I am ready for love\ Why are you hiding from me

I'd quickly give my freedom\ To be held in your captivity

I am ready for love\ All of the joy and the pain

And all the time that it takes\ Just to stay in your good grace

Lately I've been thinking maybe you're not ready for me

Maybe you think I need to learn maturity

They say watch what you ask for, cause you might receive

But, if you ask me tomorrow, I'll say the same thing

I am ready for love\ Would you please lend me your ear

I promise I won't complain\ I just need you to acknowledge I am here

If you give me half a chance, I'll prove this to you

I will be patient, kind, faithful, and true

To a man who loves music\ A man who loves art

Respects the spirit world\ And thinks with his

heart

I am ready for love\ If you'll take me in your hands

I will learn what you teach\ And do the best that I can

I am ready for love\ Here with an offering of

My voice, my eyes\ My soul, my mind

Tell me what is enough\ To prove I am ready for love"

After the last note drifted away, the apartment was eerily silent as Jeremy and Jazzy stared at one another. He jumped up suddenly and shot pass her, running into the living room. He picked up his cellphone and dialed a number as he asked Jazzy, "How understanding is your mother?"

Her face showed confusion, but she said, "Not very, but she'll listen to reason, most of the time."

When the call was answered, Jeremy said, "Clear whatever you have for tomorrow. Be at the studio around noon and don't leave until I get there." He hung up without waiting for a reply.

He turned towards Jazzy and said, "Thank you for the food. Now, go home and get some sleep." He smiled at the young, soon-to-be star, and said, "Do you know how many followers I'll get when people find out I know Jazmine Nash? Go home and pray we can convince your mother of this dream. Because, if she says yes, you start the road to stardom tomorrow!"

Chapter 14

Oh my God, thought Melody, life is so crazy. It was January now, almost two months since her debacle at the YMCA, and she couldn't be happier with her life. Well, if she could catch these burglars and make detective, she would be ecstatic. Other than that, life couldn't get any better.

Her niece, Jazmine, had become an overnight sensation. Harmony had given her blessing for Jazzy to pursue a music career, but only under one condition: She had to be managed by Chris and Jeremy, so no one could take advantage of her. Both men had readily agreed, and a week later, contracts had been signed. With a few swipes of ink, America had found its next sweetheart.

Jeremy was keeping a tight rein on Jazzy's introduction to the industry because, even though she was only 15, she looked like a grown woman. With her curvy body, her sassy attitude, and her saucy lyrics, Chris had already assigned Jazmine a permanent security team. Her social media was now handled by a publicist because, some of the messages she was receiving were down right disturbing.

But, none of the negatives even came close to the positives. Jeremy started writing for Jazmine right from the beginning. He was a genius when it came to matching a voice to a song. All the critics said she sounded like a young Tamia, with shades of Sade tossed in. Even Melody couldn't believe it was little Jazzy on the radio when one of her hits came on.

Jeremy was so connected in the entertainment world, Jazzy's sultry and rangy voice wasn't the only thing making money. He had already gotten her commercials and endorsements, and even a couple bit parts in movies.

Harmony had threatened to put an end to the whole thing over Jazmine's lack of school work. So, now, she also had a private homeschool teacher following her whenever she had to venture outside of Atlanta.

Which led to the other part of her world that was bittersweet. Her and Jeremy were closer than ever, but at the same time, so far apart. His parole officer had given him a special work exemption, and now he was spending almost everyday in some far away city promoting Jazzy. Then, when the bastard finally did come home, he'd take her out to eat or to a movie or concert, then kiss her goodnight and leave her at her door. Well, not every time, but more than she would have liked.

They talked on the phone everyday but Jeremy said he wanted to take things really slow and develop a friendship with her before thinking about a relationship. It was hard, and she didn't like being so sexually frustrated, but she also thought it was kind of sweet.

There was something else going on with Jeremy that he and his cousin were treating like a big secret. Chris had let it slip one day that Jeremy was back in town, but was only there to meet with a judge and his lawyer. She'd asked him what the meeting was about, but he'd clammed up and said it wasn't his story to tell.

A week after New Year's, after one of their funny, but sexy, phone conversations, she had asked him about his meeting with the judge. At first, he had become mad and asked why she was spying on him. Knowing both of their tempers, she calmly told him that Chris had let it slip weeks ago and now she was just asking to see if she could help in some way.

He apologized for snapping and demurely declined her

help. He said he wanted to let it play out a little before he revealed what was going on in his legal world. She accepted his right to privacy and prayed that one day he could trust her with his story.

Melody was just finishing up her shift, so she pulled the squad car into the KPD parking lot and made her way inside to clock out. She was almost to the locker room when a woman called her name. She turned to find a Junior Detective waving at her to wait. Call it intuition, but something made Melody wary.

The white, female detective told her that the Commissioner wanted her in his office, right away. Melody made her way back to the administrative offices and the Big Boss, as he was known, waved her in.

Commissioner Charlie Daniels was a 55-year-old black man with a head full of salt and pepper hair, and a clean-shaven face. Even with his huge stomach, you could clearly see he still worked out on a regular basis. He had been a Charlotte cop for 25 years before he took the job here five years ago. He was well liked, but very strict, and he demanded excellence out of every cop under his command.

In his gravelly voice, he said, "Have a seat, Officer Franklin." She had only been to his office twice before. Once to welcome her to the department, the other was for a commendation for a sizable drug bust. Once again, she couldn't explain it, but something didn't feel right.

After she was seated, he said, "I see that you are in consideration for the open Junior Detective spot. You have a very good background and more big-city experience than any other candidate. Me, having a lot of city experience myself, I know just how important that can be. How do you feel about your chances?"

Technically, the Senior Detectives Committee voted the Junior Detectives in, and the Commissioner didn't get a vote. She'd be a fool to think his input wasn't considered, though. She said, "I think I have a pretty good shot. Even if I don't get it, I'll still do my job to the best of my abilities in the future." She knew that was the right thing to say, and Comm. Daniels nodded at her answer.

He briefly shook his head and said, "You are a good cop and you have good instincts. Even after the incident last year, I still trust you to always do a good job. I really hate to see you throwing your career away over trash."

Melody's head jerked back in surprise. "I'm sorry Sir, I have no idea what you are talking about."

He leaned back in his chair, tapping a pen while he studied her. "This is a small-town, Officer Franklin. Most everything we do, the community is watching us. I can't have an officer, let alone a detective, tearing down our image in public."

Melody shrugged. "Maybe I'm just slow today. I've been putting in a lot of extra hours on these burglaries. I'm just not following you, Sir."

"I was over the Homicide Unit in the Charlotte PD before I came here. I wasn't involved in the Jeremy Harris case, but I do know he was found guilt by a jury at the end of his trial. I also know that he is on parole for the next eight years. And, I just found out that one of my officers, who says she wants to be a detective, has been seen cavorting with him all over town." He paused for a minute. "Now, how would this department look if we had a detective dating a convicted drug dealer who's out on parole?"

Melody's face burned with embarrassment. There were

clear cut rules when it came to being a cop. They couldn't tell you not to date someone with a record, but they do stipulate that, if a person is on active supervision, and it's not a spouse, the officer could be terminated.

It was a rule all cops knew because of the morals code they had to sign when hired. For some reason, she had pushed it right out of her mind. "Sir, I'm not dating Jeremy Harris. He is my neighbor and a friend. Nothing romantic is going on between us." Not by her choice, but she was telling the truth.

He nodded slowly and said, "Between me and you, Jeremy Harris is a piece of shit!"

She said, "But, after the concert at the YMCA…"

"Yeah, yeah," he said, waving it off. "I have to play nice because the mayor of Charlotte wants all of us kissing his ass because of some stunt he's trying to pull in court."

Melody couldn't resist. "What's going on in court?"

"Some nonsense about dirty cops. I don't really even care. The bottom line is, I hate that fucker. I don't care if he's your friend or your lover, I just want to make something perfectly clear to you. Are you listening?" he asked, staring into her eyes.

"Yes, Sir."

"I can't fire you without proof of some illicit affair, or wrongdoing on your part. But, I guarantee you this: As long as you are associated in any way with Jeremy Harris, you will never make detective in the KPD."

And just like that, Melody's happy days were over. How could she possibly choose between the career that defined who she was, and the man she feared she'd already fallen in love with?

Chapter 15

Jeremy was having the time of his life in Atlanta. Working with Jazmine, who was super smart, funny, and talented, breathed new life into such a depressing world. She was like a little sponge, soaking up all the knowledge he could give her. He had to admit, it felt kind of good being her mentor.

Being around Harmony was also pretty awesome. She was so beautiful on the inside and outside, he often wondered how different things would be if he had met her before Melody. Mony's warmth and strength just touched a place deep in his soul, and he found himself looking forward to the next time he could see her whenever they parted ways.

But, the truth being the truth, he enjoyed Harmony's company, but it was not romantic in the least. Melody had pretty much stolen his heart. And, romantically speaking, she was the only person he could see.

Every time he returned to Kannapolis, they would go out and have a ball. Whether it was dinner and a movie, or Go-Kart riding, they would laugh and talk and explore each other with their eyes. Normally, they would end up in front of one or the others apartment, engaging in a steamy make-out session, but Jeremy would stop it every single time.

For reasons he couldn't explain, something was telling him not to take that last step with her. If he did, disaster would strike. But they would have each other so hot and ready, they would both be sexually frustrated by the end of the night. He felt the building anticipation was something that kept them both coming back for more.

As always, though, life reared its ugly head, and he was back in Kannapolis because he had to see his parole officer in the morning.

It was 1:30am when he finally pulled up in front of his building, and all he could think about was sleep. He saw Melody's patrol car, but shook his head. He was too tired to entertain her tonight. He made his way to his apartment, took a quick shower to wash the travel off, and was asleep before his head hit the pillow.

He was awakened by a rhythmic pounding that he first thought was in his head. He looked at his phone and saw it was only 6:30am. He groaned and sat up when he realized the pounding was actually at his front door. Jeremy would have loved to just roll over and catch a few more hours of sleep, but he was excited to see the only person it could be at his door.

He threw on a pair of SKIMS for men, and some shorts, then headed to the door to let Melody in. When he opened the door, it was exactly who he knew it would be, but the expression on her face had the smile on his fading away.

Knowing something was wrong, he invited her in and headed back to his room to wash up and get dressed. Normally, she would have playfully tried to sneak peeks at him as he dressed, but when he returned ten minutes later, she was still standing by the door, arms folded across her chest, foot taping to show her irritation.

Not knowing what was wrong with her, he entered the kitchen area and said, "I was gonna call you this afternoon. I got in super late and I have to go see my probation officer at 11:00am. Can I get you something to drink?"

"Does it look like I came over here to get some coffee or juice?" she asked him with attitude.

"No. Actually, it looks like you came over here to fight.

And I have to warn you, I'm very tired and confused with this welcome. So, if you came over here for trouble, I think I'm leaning towards obliging you."

She walked over to the island separating the living area from the kitchen and leaned on it aggressively. "Do you care for me at all, or are you just having fun fucking with my head because I'm the police?"

Jeremy took a seat and rubbed a hand over his wavy hair. He took a deep breath and decided to diffuse the situation by giving her what she obviously needed. "Melody, look at me." When her eyes locked onto his, he said, "I love you, Melody. And if my actions haven't been enough to convey that to you, then I'm sorry."

A softening crossed her face, but only for a moment. Jeremy could tell she liked hearing him say those words, but she was not ready to let go of her anger just yet. "Don't play with me, Jeremy! There's no way you can love me and still keep so many secrets from me."

He frowned in confusion. "I'm not playing with you, Melody. I do love you," he told her in a soothing voice. "But, I have no idea why you're mad or what you're talking about."

"I'm talking about the fact that Comm. Daniels called me into his office yesterday and told me, as long as I was associated with you, he would make sure I never made detective."

Jeremy stood up with a glower covering his face. "That fuckin' no good piece of shit!"

Melody threw a hand up to stop his tirade. "He told me he faked being nice to you because the Mayor of Charlotte told him to. He also said it involved you trying to manipulate the courts in some way. Now, I've given you space and privacy, but now it seems I would have to throw away my career to be with you. So, basically, either you tell me why I should risk my career for you, or I won't!"

Jeremy smiled and shook his head. "I could remind you that I'm rich, and if you're with me you won't need a career, but that would make me sound selfish. I could also remind you that I just told you I love you, but that didn't seem to affect you at all the first time. So, why don't we cut the bullshit and you tell me what you want me to say or do to convince you I'm worth the sacrifice."

Finally, Melody's anger seemed to vanish. She sat down across from Jeremy and grabbed his hand between hers. "Of course, hearing you say you love me affected me. You already know I love you, too. But, if you love me, tell me this story about the dirty cops. Tell me what happened to make you hate the police so much. Tell me why the mayor of a major city would want the commissioner of the KPD to be nice to you. What I'm asking for is your trust. Because, with me, love isn't enough."

Jeremy studied her for a full five minutes. Just silently staring into her beautiful hazel eyes. Then he shrugged in an attempt to show indifference before he told her a story.

Chapter 16

The day Jeremy turned 15 years old, a new chapter opened up in his life. Being born and raised in a bad part of North Charlotte, all he knew was drugs, gangs, poverty, and violence. But, on his 15th birthday, his friend's father took him to a recording studio on North Tryon to broaden his horizon.

Even at that young of an age, Jeremy was a great singer, but an even better song writer. He liked listening to all different types of music, but the R&B scene was his main thing. After so many people lauded him for his touching and beautiful songs, he couldn't wait to hear one of them in the studio.

Before he even made it inside the building, he was hooked. In the parking lot was a Bentley, an Aston Martin, and a Rolls-Royce. If there was anything he liked more than music, it was luxury cars. When he jumped out to make his way over to the vehicles, his friend's dad grabbed him and steered him back on course to the studio.

Inside was a well-known singer and Jeremy gave him one of his songs to record. On the spot, the R&B star bought the song for $2500. He probably would have paid 20 times that amount, but at the time, Jeremy was satisfied with the pay.

From that day on, the studio was Jeremy's second home. If he wasn't in school, he was at the studio. He was there so much, they ended up giving him a job cleaning and running errands. The problem was, the studio wasn't the only attraction for him on the property.

A group of three men hung out in the parking lot all the time. Jeremy found out the guy who owned the Rolls-Royce actually owned the studio, also. Jeremy would pepper the men with questions about the music industry, but figured out soon enough, two of the men knew nothing about music beyond who their favorite rappers were. They were in another type of business altogether.

The young, light-brown skinned guy with dreads, who owned the Bentley, laughed at Jeremy one day and asked, "You think we afford dees cars off the money from a stupid ass recording studio? Man, you dumb as you look." At Jeremy's confused look, the guy said, "Dey don't call me Young Trap for no reason, if you catch my drift."

The man next to Trap gave him a pound and said, "Whaddup, Gang? You tryna school Lil Brody?" He turned and looked at Jeremy. "Dey call me J-Boa. When you tryna make dat real guap, come holla at me." He leaned back against his Aston Martin and took the blunt from the last guy in the line.

Everybody in Charlotte knew the man who owned the Rolls-Royce. He owned about 20 other luxury cars and used to be a major artist who could rap and sing. Jeremy Moore, AKA J-Murda, blew a cloud of smoke out of his mouth and said, "Your name is Jeremy, right? So is mine. I heard you got some talent with writing, and the music business can definitely get you paid. Don't listen to these knuckleheads, keep doing your thing and stay away from these streets."

Jeremy walked off, but the words of Trap and J-Boa kept repeating in his head. He was tired of seeing his mom struggle. And the fact that they had so many of his cousins living with them, only made the situation worse. A week passed before he caught Trap and J-Boa by themselves in the parking lot. Instinctively, he knew to approach them when J-Murda was close by would be a mistake.

He walked up to the two hustlers and said, "What's good, Trap? What's up, J-Boa? I need to holla at ya'll about something important."

Like always, they were passing a blunt between them while standing in front of their cars. Trap said, "What's hood, Lil Homie? You tryna hit dis Loud?"

Jeremy said, "Nah man, but I'm trying to make a little bit of money to help my moms out. How much do I need to save before I can get a pack?"

Trap and J-Boa looked at him, then each other, and fell out laughing. Every time they would stop, they would look at each other and start back laughing again. Even at 15, Jeremy wasn't a little guy. He was preparing himself to check the men for their outburst, when J-Boa started to talk.

"On Gang, dees lil niggas funny as hell. But listen bro, I respect you tryna help ya moms out, so Imma do you dis one favor. Imma sell you a thing of some Loud for $1,500, and Imma turn you on to some of the Homies so people know not to fuck wit ya money."

Jeremy pulled out $5,000 and said, "Let me get three of them and you keep the $500 for helping me out."

For the next two years, Jeremy worked hard at building up his empire. He paid off his mother's house and bought her a new car. He gave her enough money to keep the whole household fed for the foreseeable future. He also started hanging out more and more with J-Boa and Trap, the studio all but forgotten because of the draw of fast money.

When he turned 17 years old, everything got turned on its head. He was making a routine drop in his new Ford Mustang, when an unmarked cop car screamed up out of nowhere. There was nowhere to hide or run, so he knew he would take a hit for the five pounds of Exotic sitting on his backseat. Careless or just too comfortable, he had stopped hiding the drugs in the compartment under the car. That decision was about to bite him in the ass.

But something about the situation was off. The cop actually knocked on his passenger window, then got in after Jeremy unlocked the door. The man introduced himself as Det. Payne, and told Jeremy he'd been watching him for about a year at that point. He explained that he could put him away for a long time, as well as take his mother down because he was juvenile in her care when he committed the crimes.

Before the conversation could go any farther, Jeremy said, "I'm not snitching on anybody, so if you want to lock me up, then that's what it is." Jeremy also explained that he didn't live with his mother anymore, so he knew locking her up was an empty threat.

The cop sat for a minute before turning to look Jeremy in his eyes. "I'm not looking to lock you up, Jeremy Harris." With a smile on his face, Detective Payne said, "I'm trying to make both of us rich."

At Jeremy's confused look, the detective went on to explain how he and his partner had been skimming drugs off of every bust they participated in for years. They would find a buyer every now and then, but what they needed was someone who could get rid of their confiscated drugs on a regular basis.

He told Jeremy they would supply him with all the drugs and they would split the money with him, 75\25. The detective explained that they would be taking major risks by stealing the drugs and tipping him off if his name ever came up. For that, they would get the higher take.

Jeremy was skeptical of a trap, but the man had a very good talk game. Negotiations upped Jeremy's take to 40% and the partnership was solidified. The detective even gave him a crash course on selling cocaine over the next few weeks because it was new to him.

After six months, Jeremy was making more money than Trap and J-Boa combined. He moved his family out of the hood and placed them in a house in a nicer part of Charlotte. He bought his Mom a Benz G63 AMC, white with Carolina blue trim, to match the colors of her favorite sports team. He even bought a couple of Navigators for his cousins to use when they wanted to go out.

He was doing good for a few years, his silent partners warning him if his name was ever mentioned during an investigation. The detectives were providing him with so much dope, he started supplying Trap and J-Boa. They asked where he was able to get so much dope, he lied and told them he had a cousin from Philly who was looking out for him. Around that time is when everything went to shit.

Jeremy Moore, AKA J-Murda, had gotten knocked and was on his way to the FED's. He had been convicted of possession with intent to sell 80 Kilos of cocaine. The problem was, he swore to his people there was supposed to be 500 Kilos in the spot that got hit. No one knew where the dope had gone until Jeremy started putting it back on the streets without knowing it was J-Murda's dope.

Trap and J-Boa came to his spot off Sugar Creek one day, and Jeremy woke up with two guns pointed at his head.

J-Boa said, "Gang, dis when you wanna start telling da truth because, you tell one lie, Imma paint ya walls wit ya fuckin' blood, Lil Homie."

Jeremy knew they were some real gangsters, but he didn't know what this was about. Trap yelled, "Don't play dumb, mothafucka! We here about da dope. You thought you could rob da Big Homie and nobody'd find out?"

"I aint rob nobody! What the fuck, man? Ya'll know me. You know I aint robbing nobody!"

"Well, how you get J-Murda's dope? He adds a special blend to his shit, so it stands out from err body else's. He missin' 420 keys and you just hap'n to have da same dope?" asked Trap. "Fuck dat! Either start talking, or I might go to ya people's house to see if dey got it."

Jeremy blew out a breath and told them everything. He told them how the detective had approached him with the deal some years back, and he took it. He explained to them that's how he always knew when to lay low, the cop always made sure they stayed off the radar. He also made them understand that he never helped the pigs in any way, he just got the drugs, sold them, and took them their cut.

J-Boa said they would take the info to J-Murda and see what he wanted them to do. Two days later, they returned with a way for Jeremy to stay alive and atone for his bad decision. They said he would continue to sell the stolen bricks but, until J-Murda got all the money for his dope, Jeremy wouldn't keep a penny for himself.

He agreed, and for the next year, he was one of the biggest dope boys in the south, but didn't make a cent of the profit. The day he paid off J-Murda, he contacted Det. Payne and told him he was done. The cop had more threats than Mr. T on Rocky but, when it was all said and done, Jeremy never sold another drug.

A year and a half later, Det. Payne contacted him and

said they needed to meet. Jay had a lot of money put up with his family, so he didn't have to meet with the man. But, he was curious as to why the man would call him after so much time had passed. Stupidly, he went, despite his misgivings.

When he pulled into the parking lot, it was the middle of the day, so he felt like it was a safe environment. He parked where he'd been instructed, and within minutes, Detective Payne was climbing in his passenger seat.

The cop reached in his coat and pulled out a package, thick with something. He tossed it to Jeremy who caught it and looked inside. It was about three quarters of a key. The detective said, "I need you to get rid of this for me and we can split it 50\50."

Jeremy tossed the package back and told the cop to get the fuck out of his car. Det. Payne smiled and asked, "Is that your final answer?" Jeremy just stared at the man until he got out and walked away, swaggering as if he'd gotten exactly what he wanted.

That night, they raided his home and arrested him for selling to an undercover officer. They seized his house and cars and froze his bank accounts, but they never went after his family.

His bond was set at $2 Million and, even though his family could have paid it, he told them not to. Such an action would have put them on the FED's radar, more than they already were.

He went to trial and the DA played a video of Det. Payne and his partner setting up a scene made to look like they were buying drugs from him. Then, Det. Payne took the stand. He'd explained to the jury that they had been after him for years, but he had been careful until that day.

The jury took 30 minutes to bring back a guilty verdict, a record for such a big case, and Jeremy was on his way to prison.

Chapter 17

Halfway through the story, Melody got up and called in sick. Some of the story was hard to believe, but she knew she had to hear the whole thing.

By the time Jeremy was close to the end, it was nearing his appointment time. She agreed to stay put until he returned. She could tell he knew she had a lot of questions, so he told her he would answer them all when he got back.

She was laying on his huge bed, taking a nap, when she heard him calling her name from the living room. "I'm still here," she yelled from the bedroom.

He entered and stopped. "I know this isn't the time but, Melody Franklin, you are a breathtaking woman." She didn't have any sleeping clothes with her, so she had just stripped down to her bra and panties to take her nap.

She smiled and said, "There's never a wrong time to tell your woman she's beautiful."

His head cocked to the side. "Is that what you are? My woman?" She patted the bed beside her and he made his way over and laid down.

"That's a question that needs to be answered by you. I think I've made my position on the matter very clear." Before he could comment, she said, "But finish the story because, after you left, I looked Det. Payne up and it said he was killed a couple years after your arrest."

He settled in and she curled up next to him as he began to talk. "After I was found guilty, I had to go to my sentencing hearing. I was facing up to 40 years, but the minimum was 15. The Judge had showed signs of disbelief when it came to the story told by Det. Payne, so my lawyer was optimistic."

Jeremy went on to explain that he and the judge had an interesting conversation at the hearing that led to the judge giving him the 15-year minimum, then suspending over half of it. He would still have to do the whole bid, but most of it would be done on parole after his release.

"Pretty much, the whole prosecution table and police department, went crazy," Jeremy continued. "I think 20 officers ended up being charged with contempt. They were livid someone they considered a drug King-Pin was only gonna do seven years."

He explained that his lawyer went to talk to the judge after it was over and came back to Jeremy with a cryptic message. "My lawyer told me the judge said to keep my nose clean, because I probably wouldn't do the seven years he gave me."

It turned out the FBI and Charlotte PD Internal Affairs were running a mutual investigation into 12 CPD officers. Det. Payne and his partner, Det. Gibson, were part of the 12.

One too many offenders had been saying that drugs and money were missing from their stashes. Not many people would admit this for fear of more charges, but when the FBI promised immunity, the total amount of drugs unaccounted for was staggering.

"In the end," said Jeremy, "no one was willing to testify against four of the cops. So, Det. Payne and Det. Gibson walked. But the story doesn't end there."

The two detectives were emboldened by the failed investigation, and they picked up right where they had left off. That's until they ran into Mook.

Mook, AKA Raymond Green, was a young, up and coming Shot-Caller from Yonkers, New York. At 19 years of age, he was already controlling most of central North Carolina. Det. Payne and Det. Gibson thought that, if they could get their hooks into someone like him, they could retire very wealthy men.

"So, the story I got was, they busted him. A bullshit traffic violation, and Det. Payne finds ten bricks in a compartment in the trunk of his car. They made their pitch and Mook was more than happy to agree than to go to prison for life. The problem was, Mook was in a gang."

Mook kept his connection to the dirty cops a secret because he knew his Big Homies wouldn't like his involvement with them. "So, when the Bosses found out, they told him to either cut ties with the cops, or they would kill him. Mook had already been a money maker before the detectives entered the picture, so he chose to cut them off instead of going to war to keep his connect."

Melody looked confused. "Where did you get so much information? None of this is in the record."

Jeremy smiled and said, "Stop being so impatient, woman. I'm getting to that."

It was getting dark out as the sun fell below the horizon. Jeremy wrapped his arms around her and made her the little spoon as they watched the sun descend over the lake. Melody found the atmosphere very relaxing, but also very romantic. As Jeremy was doing nothing to hide his arousal at having her in his arms, it took everything in her to even care about the rest of the story.

Jeremy continued. "Det. Gibson was satisfied with the millions he had accumulated over their 10-year operation.

He tried to convince Det. Payne it was time for them to call it a day and ride off into the sunset. But Det. Payne didn't even care about the money anymore. It was personal."

Payne couldn't take the fact that Mook thought he could just walk away, but Gibson told him he was done. He was taking his ill-gotten cash, retiring, and moving to Florida. Payne asked him to help him one last time, and then they would both retire and move away. Gibson didn't like it, but he agreed to set Mook up the same way they had done with Jeremy.

They called Mook and asked him to meet them, but they were unprepared to tangle with the hardened gang member. Blood started to boil, words and threats were exchanged, and Mook ended up pulling out a gun and shooting Det. Payne in the head.

"Det. Gibson had been recording the whole encounter to use as evidence against Mook. But, when Det. Payne was shot, he cowed under a car until Mook gave up looking for him and left. They eventually caught Mook, about two months later, hiding out in New York. Before he could be extradited, the FEDs showed up to have a talk with him."

The FBI told Mook that his freedom was more than likely forever behind him, but he could help himself by helping them. They would allow him to do his time in a Federal Prison, not one of North Carolina's dreaded state institutions. They also told him they wanted the dirty cops they suspected were involved, and they'd make sure he got numbers instead of letters, if he could make that happen. He made up his mind to cooperate and tell them everything.

Det. Gibson, reading the writing on the wall, felt his time as a free man was coming to an end. He approached Internal Affairs, making a deal to bring down the rest of the dirty cops before the FEDs could reach a deal with Mook.

Melody said, "Now, I've definitely heard of this. Det. Gibson took down 25 uniforms and ten other detectives. And, because of the deal he made, all he had to forfeit was his pension. No jail time, and the bastard still retired to Florida to live the good life."

If there was one thing Melody hated, it was dirty cops. It placed a stain on the badge that the good cops had to wear, also. And, in too many cases, the dirty cops go free because the Brass didn't want the bad press.

Jeremy sensed her anger and kissed her neck before he finished the story.

"Because of Det. Gibson's confession, the FBI and IA opened all their old cases again. They started with the most severe sentences of life without parole, and are working their way forward. Believe it or not, the DA is still fighting tooth and nail to keep everyone locked up. Some of these cases have dragged on for years, the innocent languishing away in prison while people fight over politics."

Melody was confused. "How come no one has heard of all these cases being reopened? I mean, you're a star. This should be all over the news!"

Jeremy pulled her closer and said, "A lot of guys want to keep this on the low because of the target that will fall on them for working with the cops. Look at Mook's situation. A big number of these guys are in gangs, or some other form of organized crime. Their people won't care that the cops were dirty, they'll kill them for having any dealings with the police."

"So, in the interest of keeping the inmate\victim safe, the state put a gag order over the whole thing?" Melody guessed.

"That's right," confirmed Jeremy.

"So, why does the mayor of Charlotte want everyone kissing your ass?"

That's when Jeremy dropped the bombshell. "Because the verdict in my case comes down next week. And, with everyone pretty much knowing the outcome, I won't be a convicted felon anymore." He paused for a second. "And it also might have a little something to do with the $500 Million lawsuit my lawyer brought on the city of Charlotte, and the State of North Carolina."

Chapter 18

Jeremy was now truly a free man. No parole. No restrictions. No more felon status. His conviction had been overturned, with prejudice, and a crowd of his supporters had unleashed a huge cheer in the courtroom. The DA had been damn near crying because, now, Jeremy's lawsuit was pretty much in the bag.

He and Chris were in his Ferrari heading to the club they had reserved for a night of dancing and celebrating. Jeremy had been getting congratulatory calls and text all day from family and friends, most of which were at the club waiting on his arrival.

A couple of rap stars that he'd wrote songs for had already bought out the bar, and promised to perform some hits for the attendees. Jeremy knew it would be packed; nothing brought people out more than free entertainment and free alcohol.

Jeremy was beside himself with happiness, and he was looking forward to celebrating with his people. But, he couldn't help the anticipation that flooded his system when he thought about the private afterparty he had planned with Melody.

The night he'd told her what was going on with his case, they had talked about what they could do to celebrate his clean record. It had led to a heavy make-out session, and a promise of a heated night following his updated status. They had slept naked in each other's arms for the first time that night. All it did was inflate the fire that was already burning inside them both.

She had taken the day off to be in the courtroom to support him, and would also be at the party with Harmony and Jazzy, who was also slated to perform. But Melody would be leaving early to set the scene for their private celebration back at his place. He told her all he needed was her, but she had been adamant about starting their relationship off with a bang.

They hadn't told anyone about their new committed status, so Chris was in the car listing all of the fine women who would be at the club.

"Jennifer is gonna be there. You know, the one that stayed up the block from you? Looks like Serena. I know you been after her since high school. Let's see, Chasity and her two cousins, Cece and Sequoia, gonna be there. Now, Chasity aint the same little Chasity you remember. She thick as hell, but still pretty in the face. Then we got Toni and Shelly. Shonda and Tosha…"

"Hey! Hey! Hey! Okay, I get it," said Jeremy, cutting off the tirade. "There's gonna be a lot of fine ass women. I understand. But, I'm not checking for none of them."

Chris jerked his head back in disbelief. "Man, I'm starting to get worried about you. First, you didn't want the triple deluxe I set up for you when you got out. Then, you had all them dimes in Atlanta throwing it at you, but you turned them all down. Unless you got something in the cut, you aint hit shit since you been out. What? You hitting Chanel? She fine as hell, but she crazy as shit!"

Jeremy huffed out a breath. "Cuz, I'm 30 years old. I'm not a little boy anymore, running around trying to see up girls' skirts. I'm taking care of my business and my responsibilities. Anyway, when I do go looking, I'm looking for something real. Not some cheap thrill for the night."

Chris dropped his head, then looked at Jay with concern

on his face. "Did those boys touch you in the Pen? Did one of them do something to your manhood? Cause you sound like a little bitch right now."

Jay stopped at a light about a block from the club, and turned to his amused cousin with a deadly expression. "Chris, I love you man. I don't know where I'd be in life without you. But, I'm gonna say this, and I want to be clear so you understand." After a pregnant pause, he said, "Don't ever joke about shit like that with me. You have no idea the stuff that goes on in prison. The stuff I've seen…" His voice floated away and all he could do was shake his head and proceed to the club.

When they pulled up to valet parking, Chris said, "Little cousin, I'm sorry for dampening the mood. Don't let my ignorance ruin your day. You've been after your freedom since you turned 15-years-old. Now it's yours. I just want you to have a good time and enjoy the life you've built for yourself."

"I know, Chris." Jeremy studied the front of the club, then glanced at him and said, "Don't worry about me. And just to let you know, I already got a little something lined up for the night."

Chris looked unconvinced. "Who? And you better not tell me you done went Hollywood and got you a white girl!"

Jeremy smiled as he opened his door. "Nah, I went one better." Looking back over his shoulder, he said, "I got me a cop!"

As he exited the low-slung car, he heard his cousin say, "Well aint that bout a bitch?" before they shared a good laugh and entered the club together.

Chapter 19

Jeremy and Chris were having the time of their lives. A couple of NC's finest entertainers had shown up, and the club was packed with people enjoying life and celebrating Jeremy's victory.

Since the party was strictly invite only, Jeremy knew pretty much everyone in the building. From childhood friends, to colleagues, to family. Everyone was dancing and drinking, some were even getting their freak on.

Security was very laidback, most of them never even ventured inside the building. With so much alcohol flowing, and so many young, attractive, rich people, they had to be called in a couple times when someone's exhibitionist display got a little too graphic. Other than that, everyone was in a chill mood, just trying to celebrate life.

When Jeremy and Chris first entered the club, they'd been wearing thick, insulated coats to combat the cold night. But, it was so hot inside the bash, pretty quickly, they were both dancing around in black wife-beaters.

A shirtless Jeremy was in one of the VIP bathrooms washing the sweat from his body, when he heard the door open and close behind him. He had his head under the water, but distinctly heard the sound of the lock engaging. He toweled off his face just as the lights dimmed to a soft glow. Out of the shadows emerged an Angel, dressed all in white.

Angel wasn't the right description for the vision in front of him. More like a sexual goddess. Dressed in a white, stretchy, halter top that stopped bare inches below her swelling chest, she had her flat and sexy midriff on full display. Officer Melody Franklin paused and posed, hip cocked to the side. He groaned, salivating for a taste of her sculpted body.

Neither said a word as he continued his examination of this extremely erotic woman. His eyes damn near popping out of his head with the heat building up in his body.

Her nails were freshly manicured. Her juicy, pink lips glistened invitingly. Her dark, crinkly hair cascaded around her well-toned shoulders, and he was struck immobile by her spectacular beauty.

A pair of high waisted, white pants, made from some soft, pliable material, conformed to the contours of her amazing hips, legs, and perfect ass. To complete the ensemble, the pants were tucked into knee high, silver, stiletto boots that made her legs appear to be a mile long.

Finally, she took a couple steps closer, sashaying with the confidence of a woman who knew she looked dazzling. She said, "I just had a very interesting conversation with your cousin, Chris. He informed me that you've been celibate since you came home." As she talked, she kept taking small, swaying steps towards him, making it painfully obvious that she wasn't wearing a bra.

"I thought to myself," Melody continued, "what about all those women who have been throwing themselves at him? My next thought was that, our night could be very short if you didn't have something to take the edge off first. So, I want you to shut up, stay still, and let me prepare you for our special night."

By the time she said the last word, she was standing about an inch away from him, and he was already throbbingly erect. Her passion fruit scent was making him dizzy with desire as he tried to get his mind and mouth to function properly. "Melody, I…"

"Shhhh," she commanded, laying a finger across his lips. "No talking. And keep your hands on the countertop behind you. Just relax and enjoy."

Jeremy had known Melody wasn't a shrinking violet. Based on past experiences, he knew she had a very healthy sexual appetite. But, the role of seductress was new to him. He now knew that, the last few months, she'd been taking it easy on him. Without even touching him in a sexual way, she had awakened a lust in him that he'd never known in his life. He was losing control, but he found himself thrilled with the feeling.

She started by planting a small kiss on his naked chest. Then, she ran her tongue over both his nipples, forcing his head to fall back on his shoulders. She used her small teeth to leave teasing bite marks all over his chest. Then, her tongue would dart out, soothing away the sting after each playful bite.

Her moist lips started to move up at the same time her arms encircled his neck, pulling his head down so he could meet her eyes. She molded her soft body to his, then sealed their mouths in a searing union. As they kissed, deeply and passionately, their tongues went on a journey of each other's souls. She tasted so good, and the friction of her undulations against his manhood had him ready to unleash in his sweatpants.

No amount of alcohol had ever made him drunk like this. She unwound her arms, but kept the kiss going strong, using her nails to rake down his sculpted chest. When her hands reached his waistband, one hand pulled the front loose, the other went digging for gold.

When her small fingers wrapped around him, she squeezed so hard, he broke the kiss and said, "Oh God,

Melody! Hold up! You have to stop…"

She stroked him one time, from root to tip, and back again before saying, "Jeremy, I thought I told you no talking? I won't tell you again. If you want me to stop, just say another word and I'll leave." Like any man in the world, crazy or sane, he chose to shut up. But Melody didn't. She decided to stoke the flames a little with her words.

"Good. Now, what I'm going to do is give you a little relief," she explained. "Because, once I get you back to the apartment, I expect to be pleased well into the morning. Do I make myself clear? A nod with suffice." While she was giving her speech, her hand started playing a slow tune between his legs. Not having a choice, he tried to keep his legs locked, and nodded his head.

Her mouth went back to work. She kissed an unhurried, sensual path down his body, making a beeline towards his hardness. After a few seconds, she was sitting back on her hunches, looking up at his face. Without warning, in one motion, she used both of her hands to pull his pants and underwear down to his ankles.

His breathing kicked up drastically as his freed manhood waved in the air, inches from her glossy lips. Their eyes were still locked until, leisurely, she let her gaze travel down the length of his body. He could almost feel when her gaze finally landed on his erection.

She said, "So, you haven't been with anyone in over seven years?" He frantically shook his head. "And you haven't climaxed in all that time?" Again, he shook his head. "No self-gratification?" Another headshake. She smiled and blew a warm breath on him, producing a long hiss from his lips. Melody gave a devilish giggle and said, "Um, um, um! This is gonna be fun."

Jeremy was not small by anyone's measure. Looking down at Melody's slick mouth, he wasn't sure he was gonna fit. She wrapped her warm hand about halfway down his shaft, triggering a low growl from deep in his throat.

She gave one last saucy smile, then began to lick all over him like a melting ice cream cone. He fought hard to keep his eyes open because he didn't want to miss any of the show. Every now and then, her eyes would shoot up to his face, he guessed to make sure he was watching her impressive performance.

Then, without warning, she wrapped her lips around the head, sliding forward until her velvety mouth met her hand. Without conscious thought, his head fell back again. She immediately pulled off of him, and said, "Look at me!"

His head snapped back forward and she squeezed him hard, giving him a sinful look before setting her mouth back to work.

He was not gonna last much longer with the way things were going. But, even that time was reduced when her hand started pumping, making his body stiff all over.

Something in his face or posture must have given away the fact that he was on the brink, because her eyes took on a mischievous quality, and her hand dropped away from him. Then, it was a roller coaster ride to the end.

His eyes bugged out of their sockets when she started taking deep dives down his maleness. She was going so fast, and so deep, he thought he would pass out from the pleasure. When he felt his tip touch the back of her throat, the feeling pushed him over the edge.

He started shivering and shaking as the first warm surge shot into her wet heat. She groaned as if savoring his flavor as he continued to flood her mouth with his sticky fluids.

Finally, after what felt like an eternity, she drained him and began to lick him clean. She pulled back up his pants and underwear, then tucked him safely back inside. Without another word, she walked off, leaving him struggling to remain standing, watching her in awe.

At the door, she released the lock and opened it up. The light from the hallway illuminated the heavenly lips that had just given him so much pleasure. She looked back over her shoulder and, with love in her eyes, whispered, "I'll see you when you get home." Then she was gone.

Chapter 20

Jeremy was done with this stupid ass party. He was scowling at all the people who were still milling about, trying to find a lover, or at least one more drink. His cousin had left a while ago with some blue eyed, pale-ass, dark haired, white chick that had came with one of the rappers. So now, it was close to 2:00am, and he was stuck looking stupid.

After Melody left the bathroom, she had disappeared. And if the party wasn't for him, he would have been right behind her. But that had been around 10:00pm. Now, all these motherfuckers hanging around were just pissing him off.

Other than the obvious, the highlight of the evening had been Jazzy's performance. She had come out around 12:00am, pretty much bringing the house down. She had sung one of her more upbeat numbers, and had grown men dancing and singing her music in the club. So far, all her hits had been written by him, but he was encouraging her to use her talents and start writing for herself.

After Jazzy finished, he met her and Mony in a quiet back office where he congratulated her on a job well done. They both in turn congratulated him for exonerating himself. Mony glided over to him and kissed him loudly on his lips. She said, "I won't be able to do that after tonight from what I heard. So, congrats on that, too." They headed back to Atlanta, but her words made him all too aware of what was waiting for him at home.

Gritting his teeth, he finally had to start ushering some of the stragglers towards the door. He smiled and laughed with them, but ultimately lead them out of the building. By

2:30, the last of the guest were leaving, and he was waving bye to the club's manager.

His apartment was maybe an hour away in a normal car on a normal night. This late, and in the mood he was in, he pushed the Ferrari to try and cover the distance in 30 minutes. But he still had to be careful. With his victory in court, it would please the city of Charlotte to no end to lock him up for reckless driving. So, he split the difference and made it back in 40 minutes, only speeding up once he got out of Mecklenburg County.

When he pulled up in front of his apartment, he admitted he was a little afraid. Melody had just given him the most pleasure he'd had in his life. He was a little worried he would disappoint her. But it damn sure wasn't gonna stop him from trying to return the favor.

He exited his vehicle and found that, in his rush to leave the club, he'd forgotten to grab his coat. Damn that coat, he thought. He planned to get so hot tonight, he would never need another coat in his life.

It seemed like the elevator was taking all day, but he would have to go around the side of the building to get to the steps. So, he waited it out. Finally, the door opened and he rushed to scan his card to get the thing moving.

He knew he needed to slow down. He hadn't been this horny since Chasity use to wear those skimpy outfits and tease him in school. But, how was Melody to know she hadn't cooled his jets at all. In fact, he would probably climax the second he laid eyes on her wet and willing body.

Jeremy let himself into the apartment quietly, taking care not to make any unnecessary noise. Melody had been there for hours and, if he could, he wanted to wake her up in the best way possible. He peeked into his bedroom and, sure enough, she was laid out on his bed, dead to the world.

She hadn't been sleeping the whole time, though. He could hear one of his biggest hits playing softly in the background. The curtains were pulled back and the moonlight made the room glow. Scented candles were burning, filling the whole apartment with her wonderful fragrance. She had created the perfect atmosphere for two new lovers who wanted to make lasting memories on their first night together.

He slowly walked over to the bed and took a deep inhale of the woman he loved. She'd kept the all white theme going, but the delicate light coming in over the lake made the diaphanous material transparent. Her dark brown nipples, and the deep V between her thighs, were covered, but the flimsy garment left nothing to the imagination.

Her mouth-watering aroma caused him to become aware that his own smell left a lot to be desired. He cast one last look at her, then retreated to the guest portion of his home.

He took a shower and used the Old Spice Nightpanther bodywash that he knew drove her crazy. He stepped into the silent wind dryer and then padded naked back to his bedroom where Melody was still sleeping.

Jeremy felt like a voyeur, but he couldn't help himself. He had seen her naked plenty of times, and had even curled up with her skin to skin. But, on those occasions, he hadn't been about to make love to her. Now, he surveyed her body from across the room as he mapped out exactly what he was about to do to her.

He had to be careful as he ventured over to the bed. He

was painfully erect, and he feared that too much stimulation would have him coming before he even got started.

Jeremy eased himself onto the bed between her outstretched legs and lifted the almost nonexistent gown to bare her lower body to his view. Her lower lips were plump and, because she was expertly clean shaven, he could see the pinkness that awaited him on the inside.

He eased his head down and blew a soft breath over her mound. She responded with a slight dampening and a quiet moan. He blew warm breath over her once again and she moaned deeper as her flower parted and became moist.

Her womanly musk mixed perfectly with the fruitiness of her perfume, an intoxicating blend that filled his nostrils as well as his soul. It was time to wake his sleeping Queen and get this party started. He extended his tongue and traced her outer lips softly until her hips stated to rotate with his motion. Then he stabbed deep into her core, forcing her to gasp and wake up, unleashing a small, "Ooooh! Yes!"

His strong arms pushed her hips back to the bed as his tongue continued to torment her flame. He kept his strokes deep at the bottom of her pit, but brought it closer to the surface the closer he got to her hidden pearl. As soon as it revealed itself, he reached up and latched onto her erect nipples, at the same time his lips locked onto her clit.

She quivered and screamed as he increased the suction, bringing about her first climax of the night. He let go of her breasts and pushed her knees all the way up to her chest, using his tongue to capture all the fluids gushing out of her core. It tasted so good, he made a scoop with his mouth and dipped to the bottom of her treasure to make sure he got it all.

He wasn't done with her by a long shot, and he wasn't letting her come back down yet, either. He moved his mouth back up to her swollen nub and started flicking it as fast as he could. He also took one of his long, wide fingers and pushed it deep inside her womanhood.

Jeremy was searching for something. He kept making a 'come here' movement with his finger until her chest started heaving and her breath came rapidly. She screamed, "Ahhh! Yes! Jeremy! Don't stop. Ughhh God!"

Her legs started to tremble, his hand and face glistened with her nectar. He alternated between flicking with his tongue and sucking forcefully on her clit. Then his finger found the spot he'd been skimming for.

She screamed again and tried to scramble away. He grabbed her legs to halt her retreat, and used his nail to scape the spot that caused her to go crazy. She was now shaking uncontrollably, trying unsuccessfully to push his head away from her wetness. But, he was too strong and too pleased with the pleasure he was bringing her.

All at once, her body became stiff as a board. She gave a hoarse cry and released a flood all over his hand, his face, and the bed. He put his whole mouth over her lower lips and kept swallowing until the flood became a drip, then the drip faded and her body finally went lax.

Chapter 21

Most men would probably have stopped there and took their own pleasure, but Jeremy was on a mission to make this the best night of her life. She was staring up at the ceiling with a loose-jointed satisfaction that made him chuckle deeply. While her body was so pliant, he removed her gown and went back to pleasing her.

This time, he wanted to map out all of her delectable contours and leave her begging for him to take her. He moved down to his Queen's feet. He kissed each of her heels, then bathed her feet and toes with his hungry mouth.

He traveled a bit higher and kissed, licked, and sucked all over her calves until he had her moaning once again. He glanced up at her face, the look she was giving him almost made him abandon his mission and sink into her right there and then. But, he wanted to taste every inch of her body and let her know that she now belonged to him.

By the time he reached her thighs, she was brushing her fingers over his hair, hissing every time his lips encountered one of her spots. His tongue again explored her pubic area, but this time, he didn't touch her lower lips at all. She was trying to drag his face where she wanted it while rotating her hips, but he had another destination in mind that had been driving him crazy since day one.

Jeremy knew that Melody was 30 years old. He had no idea when nature would rear its ugly head and start working on her womanly body. But Melody's voluptuous, perky breasts had to defy some kind of natural law.

He blew on her fully erect nipples; her shivering caused the plump beauties to jiggle enticingly. Her silver dollar sized areolas were the same dark chocolate color of her nipples, and he had to see if they tasted as good as they looked. So, he settled his torso between her splayed thighs to anchor her body, then he nursed at her beautiful mounds.

He alternated from one to the other. Sometimes locking on with a strong suction, other times letting his tongue flick back and forth like he'd done with her clit. Every now and then, he would roll the tightened bud between his teeth, resulting in her arms forming a death grip on his head. He settled in on a combination that had her hunching his torso until she had a soft, but effective, orgasm.

He moved up her body until he was looking directly into her eyes. In a voice laced with lust, he said, "If you feel as good as you taste, I won't last very long." After a long, lingering kiss, he asked, "Are you ready for me?" She nodded her head, still somewhat in a daze. Heart thumping with anticipation, he placed the tip of his steel at the entrance of her tunnel, but quickly locked their gazes before he started to push.

"Ahhh…. Ooooh! Yes!" she said, a fresh gush of liquid splashed his manhood. He initiated a smooth back and forth motion, each forward stroke allowing him to sink a little deeper than the one before.

"Ooooh! Shit!" Jeremy said through clinched teeth. Her furnace was burning him alive. Her sheath was molten hot, wet silk, that was squeezing him so tight, he had to stop moving or he would go off before he was all the way in.

"No, Jeremy! Don't stop!" she demanded, wrapping her legs around him and drumming her heels on his ass. He gritted his teeth and tried to think about baseball as he picked his rhythm back up. After two more forced pauses to gather himself, his patient thrusts paid off. He felt the head of his stiffness meet the spongy firmness of her cervix.

He crafted a slow, rotational grind that made Melody's mouth fall open and her eyes roll back into her head. She came with another scream, and there was nothing he could do to stop his own tide from flowing.

Her walls flooded him with lava, pulsing around him, forcing him to moan and release deep inside of her. Her muscles continued to milk him as convulsions ripped through both of their bodies. He fell heavily on her, but quickly rolled them both so she ended up on top.

Breathing heavy and glistening with sweat, he stroked his hands up and down her back, her internal grip on him finally relaxing. They both became aware of his still-aroused state at the same time. She lifted her hips in a long, lazy shift until she reached the very tip of him. Then, she slammed herself downward, engulfing his soaked member.

The sensations were too much for either of them and they both groaned out loud. But Melody repeated the same, slow ascent. This time, though, ending it with an almost violent descent. She did it again and again. To keep his sanity intact, Jeremy was forced to grab her ass cheeks to stop the torture.

She tried to fight his hold, but he was using all his strength to keep her still. In a voice that sounded demonic in its origin, she demanded, "Let! Me! Go!" He continued to hold her, struggling to maintain control, but she came up with a new method of torture.

He could feel their combined juices all over his thighs as her inner muscles started to undulate around his shaft. He gasped, figuring it was pointless to continue trying to hold her; either action would force another climax out of him. So, he released her buttocks, and she immediately went back to work.

Her knees were already bracketing his hips, so she sat up, braced her hands on his chest, and gave him a fierce look. Their eyes locked, and he could honestly say that he had never seen a more magnificent woman in his life. They both knew that this would be the finale for round one, so Jay laid back and let Melody take them home.

She began a slow rotation of her hips that used his shaft like a stir-stick for her pleasure. As he was buried deep in her womb, he could feel his tip once again massaging her cervix. After a couple minutes of this, he was gripping the sheets, toes curling into claws.

He was watching her face the whole time, privileged to witness the myriad of emotions playing out in her eyes. Then, she developed a faraway look that told him she was reaching a whole new level of passion.

All of a sudden, Melody started jerking her hips erratically back and forth, whispering his name over and over. As the tempo increased, so too did her volume. He was fighting to keep his eyes open as she switched from the grind to bouncing up and down as hard and fast as she could. Her hands left his chest as she leaned back for a deeper penetration, revealing her sensational body to his gaze.

Her hands settled behind her on his thighs; her head fell back as she began her erratic grinding again. Her climax caused her whole body to spasm as her essence shot out all over his stomach and thighs. She screamed his name in her moment of total bliss.

It was over. Jeremy lifted them both off the bed with his jerking hips as she drained him of every fluid left in his body. She fell on his chest and that's where they laid for the next ten minutes, regaining their strength and clutching one another.

Finally, Jeremy sat up and swung his feet to the floor. Melody wrapped her body tightly around his and mumbled a protest when he stood up. He carried her into the shower where he reluctantly allowed his body to slip from hers, which brought a shiver from them both.

He turned the water on and they spent a rejuvenating 15 minutes getting cleaned up. Jay exited first and quickly stripped the linens off the bed so his lady wouldn't have to lay on soiled sheets.

She stood, proudly naked, in the bathroom doorway as he made the bed fresh again. She said, "I don't know why you're doing that? I'm not done with you yet." Just hearing her say that brought him back to full hardness. But, he pulled on a pair of shorts and threw her a long T-shirt before sitting down on the side of the bed.

"I'm sorry, Melody. I got so carried away, I never said anything about protection."

She laughed and said, "If the result of what we just did is a baby, all that would do is extend the pleasure even longer. At least, after I curse you during the birth."

His head jerked up and he said, "You want to have my children?"

She walked over and stood between his legs. She kissed him lightly and said, "I want whatever you are willing to give me. Your children. Your heart. Your love." She paused to make sure he was listening. "Your last name."

Their eyes bore into each other's as he said solemnly, "Melody, I can't ask for your hand," causing her to frown and her head to drop. "Until I meet your parents and buy you a ring," he continued with a smile.

She squealed and jumped on his lap, which pushed them back onto the bed. Her prediction proved to be right. About two hours later, they were taking another shower and he was once again changing the sheets.

Chapter 22

Jeremy woke that Saturday afternoon at 3:30 to the sound of Melody talking on her phone from the kitchen area. She was talking excitedly, his instinct telling him it was her sister on the line. She was trying to be quiet, but it was clear she was overjoyed about something. He smiled, hoping the delight had something to do with him.

Jeremy was wiped out. They had made love so many times during the night and early morning, he hadn't planned on getting out of bed until tomorrow. But his pride wouldn't let him lay around while his woman was up and about.

Before he could sit up, he heard the tenor of Melody's conversation change. She now sounded more professional, and he clearly heard her say, "Yes, Sir. I'm on my way," before going silent.

She rushed into the bedroom and, seeing him awake, said, "I'm sorry if I woke you, sweetie. I had to tell my sister the good news." She leaned over and gave him an earth scorching, good morning kiss before backing away from his seeking hands.

"Sorry babe, but my partner called and we finally caught a break on those burglaries. We're executing a warrant on the suspects in about 30 minutes. I still have to get dressed, so I have to go." She gave him one more kiss and let his hands roam over her ass and hips before laughing and pulling back.

At the door, she looked back and said saucily, "Honey, make sure you get some rest. I know I wore you out last night." He faked like he was gonna jump up and chase her, so she ran out of the room, yelling, "I love you," over her shoulder.

Jeremy heard the door close and thought, fuck it, he was still tired. He pulled the blankets back over his body and drifted off to sleep with the smell of passion fruit in his nose.

He had no idea how long he slept, but when the pounding finally pulled him from sleep, it was dark outside. He grabbed his cell phone and noticed that he had 32 missed calls and 50 unread text messages. He regarded the time, 11:08pm, and wondered why so many people were searching for him on a Saturday night.

Then he remembered the pounding at his front door. He figured Melody had forgotten the key he'd given her, and was trying to get back in. He jumped up and put on a pair of shorts and made his way to the door, a teasing smile etched across his face.

When he opened the door, he immediately pulled his body back behind it. Harmony was standing in the hallway and, after a brief examination, it was clear that she had been crying. Forgetting his shorts-only clad body, he swung the door out of the way and grabbed her hands, pulling her into the apartment.

"What's wrong, Harmony? I thought you went back to Atlanta? Where's Jazzy? Did something happen to Jazzy?" She shook her head as fresh tears flooded her eyes.

"Not Jazzy," was all she could get out before she broke down into a soul wrenching cry.

On instinct, he grabbed her and dragged her small body against his own. He remembered when he had cried and she had offered him comfort, so he wrapped her up and murmured as he rubbed her back. Then her words penetrated the fog of his brain.

Jeremy softly pulled back and lifted her chin so he could

look into her eyes. "If nothing is wrong with Jazmine, then what are you crying for? What's wrong with you?"

She looked deep into his eyes and said, "Jeremy, I'm so sorry. I've been trying to reach you for hours, and I felt like I had to be the one to tell you. So, I drove back up from Atlanta…" She paused, shaking her head as if she couldn't bear to continue.

He stared at her as a deep dread crept into his soul. "Drove up here to tell me what? And where is Melody?"

"I'm sorry Jeremy, but I received a call earlier that Melody was shot and killed this afternoon, about 4:00, while serving a warrant." She reached for him but he roughly pushed her arms away.

"No," said Jeremy, softly. "Why would you say something like that?" He turned and said, "Let me get my phone. I'll call her right now."

He took one step and Harmony shouted, "JEREMY!" He spun back around, alarmed by the normally soft-spoken woman's shout. Her face crumpled and he read the truth in her expression when she said, "Jeremy, she's gone."

"No! No!" he yelled. Tears flooded his eyes as he backpedaled, saying, "No!" over and over again. Finally, he fell to his knees and screamed out his anguish. He plummeted all the way to the ground and curled up, saying, "She's not gone! I just found her. She can't be gone. I need her!"

He was vaguely aware that Harmony was curled up around his body, crying with him. When he briefly surfaced from the black hole he'd fallen in, he was laying in his own bed, his mother hovering by his side. He didn't remember getting up from the floor, or really even what day it was. All he knew was the misery and pain from knowing that Melody was truly gone.

He rolled over and pulled the pillow to his face that still held a trace of her scent, letting the pain consume him. He drifted off with memories of his Queen overpowering his senses. His last thought was, he had to do something with his life to honor the person who saved his: Officer Melody Franklin.

Epilogue

Jeremy watched the movers place the last of his belongings in the truck, then slam the back door. He and Chris leaned on the front of his Range Rover as they watched the truck pull off to start its long journey to his new home.

"I know you're hurting right now little cousin, but when you're ready, you know your family will always have your back." Chris accompanied his declaration with a soft pat of his shoulder.

Jeremy just looked at his cousin, his friend, and smiled. The last two months had been hell on Jeremy. Melody's funeral had placed a black cloud around his life and only the love of his family had been able to pull him out.

He had met Joe and Whitney Franklin the day before the funeral, and they'd treated him like the Son-in-law he had been destined to become.

Jeremy looked at Chris and said, "I wasted so much time, man. I really only had the one night with her. I'm fucked up, Cuz. I can't close my eyes without seeing her face." He dropped his head as the tears started to fall. They always did whenever he dwelled on the love of his life.

Chris didn't offer any platitudes, or downplay his feelings. He just patted his shoulder and gave a little squeeze, remaining silent in the presence of his sorrow.

Melody had been the one to find the clue that ultimately led to the identification of the burglars. In response, the Captain of the SWAT team had allowed her to suit up and join them on the takedown. When the door was hit, the three occupants scattered like the roaches they were.

She had run one of the men down and tackled him, but

the suspect pulled a gun from his waist. They were wrestling for the gun when it went off, sending a bullet threw her neck. It severed her main artery and Melody had pretty much died instantly. There was nothing the EMTs could do.

When Jeremy had himself together, he said, "I guess I better get on the road." He had settled his case with the city of Charlotte and the state for $200 Million. He had already been rich, but now he didn't have a worry in the world. So, now he was moving to Atlanta to be close to Harmony and Jazzy. But also, to be near Melody's gravesite.

He hugged his cousin and they exchanged goodbyes as Jay hopped in his vehicle. He didn't know what the future would hold. He didn't know how long his mourning period would last. But, he knew the rest of his life would be devoted to spreading the love that Melody had opened up inside of his heart.

As he got on the highway heading south, he smiled as he felt a warmth surround his body. Ever since Melody's death, he'd get these warm feelings out of nowhere. He liked to think it was Melody letting him know that she was still by his side. He turned on the radio, hoping something would be playing that would perk up his melancholy mood.

"Your number one Hip-Hop and R&B station, bringing you nothing but the new hotness for your drive to work. This next joint is already at the top of every chart in America. If anyone can explain to me how a 16-year-old girl could put so much emotion into a song, please call me and do so.

"Well, without further ado, I want to introduce the number one song in the world right now, *PERFECT MELODY*. Written by the award-winning Jeremy Harris, and performed by the sensational superstar, Jazmine Nash."

THE FIRST VICTIM

L. A. BURCH

THE FIRST VICTIM

Before the messages. Before the investigations and inquiries. Before anyone could guess at a motive or who the next victim would be: THERE WAS A FIRST!

But who was he? Why was he chosen? What made him important? Was there a reason for this pick, or was it just bad luck on the victim's part?

Take a glimpse into the Mastermind world and see if you can solve the riddles. Is the killer truly insane? Or, is there a method to his madness that only the supremely gifted can see? Read *The First Victim* and form your own conclusions.

When you think you have everything figured out, pick up *Retribution: Book One Of The Masterminds Series*. You'll quickly see that the answers are more complex than you thought.

The Beginning

Former Officer Trevor Jones awoke five minutes ago to discover an aspiration that every single human being should add to their long- and short-term plans: Never wake up in the trunk of a car. To add insult to injury, he was in the trunk of his own car. He knew this because, every time the bastard driving his car turned a corner, or hit a rut in the road, one of the tools he used in his carpentry business stabbed him in his side.

To make matters worse, Trevor wasn't even sure how he'd gotten into his trunk. The last he could remember, he'd been putting the finishing touches on a massive oak desk he planned to use in his home office. He had just turned on the wall-mounted LED lights to replace the waning sunlight that usually filtered in through the numerous windows and skylights in the garage. Then…Nothing.

He couldn't remember an intruder, or an attack that would've rendered him unconscious. On top of that, he had no pain in his body that spoke of a sustained injury. He would have loved to run his hands over his body just to make sure, but two minutes ago, he discovered something even more spine-chilling than waking up in the trunk of his own car. How about waking up in the trunk of your own car, in pitch-blackness, and not being able to move a muscle?

Trevor could hear the tires screaming over the asphalt of whichever road his abductor was driving on. He could feel his work uniform of jeans, t-shirt, and boots brushing his skin with the swaying motion of the car. He could even smell the gas, the rubber, and the faint electrical scent that's associated with a speeding car on the open road.

He could faintly perceive the occasional overhead light

1

flash by the minute openings around the trunk's lid. And he could definitely taste the mixture of fear and trepidation on his tongue. So, all his senses seemed to be in working order. But, even though he could feel no restraints on his body, no matter how hard he tried, he couldn't move an inch.

Being a 50-year-old black man who grew up in the foothill's region of North Carolina, Trevor had felt dread a few times in his life. The first time he'd come face to face with several KKK members and heard the delighted cackles that accompanied their discovery, he had only been 7-years-old, but something visceral whispered in his mind of mortal danger. He had turned and fled from the park as fast as his young body would take him, even as the urine streamed down his pumping legs.

Back then, he hadn't really understood how much danger he'd been in. His body had responded on instinct to a situation that he could barely comprehend. That wasn't the case now. As a grown man, he could at least hold his bladder, for the time being anyway. But the thought running through his mind, put him in a panicked, frenzied state.

Trevor's love of horror movies turned out to be a detriment in this situation. Every knife wielding, chainsaw slinging, blood-thirsty serial killer appeared in his mind in vivid detail. His breathing kicked up a notch as he envisioned the soulless monstrosity that would be revealed once the lid opened. Would it be some type of otherworldly creature? Or one of those KKK men returning for the entertainment he'd deprived them of all those years ago?

Reasonable or not, his mind was churning out every gruesome death he'd ever seen in one of those movies while his Honda Accord continued towards its eventual destination.

After allowing his imagination to wander unchecked for a few minutes, he deepened his breaths and tried to slow his galloping heart. He needed to think! There had to be a real reason why someone would remove him from his home and transport him to an undisclosed location. If the person, or people, wanted him dead, they could have ended his life in the garage. For sure, no one would have come looking for his corpse until he missed his child support payment.

Trevor had lived alone ever since he lost his job as a correctional officer at Foothills Youth Institution. When word got out that he'd been starving the boys during their stay in Restrictive Housing, his pregnant wife had packed him a bag, tossed it out on the porch, and told him he needed to find another place to stay.

With one-year-old Trevor Junior on her hip, and Makayla only two months away from being born, his wife had marched into court, demanded full custody of the children, and was rewarded a child support amount that would keep him in debt until the kids turned 18. That had been 16 years ago, and he'd lived alone in the two-bedroom home, with the ramshackle yard, ever since.

Being the hypocrites they were, even though the community always had bad things to say about the animals being housed in their backyard, he was still the city's pariah after all this time. So, he had no money. Nothing of any value, except maybe his tools. Maybe it was a relative of one of those inmates coming back to exact some revenge! After a second, he dismissed the thought as ludicrous. That would mean the culprit had been waiting for almost twenty years.

Robbery as a motive didn't make sense either. His house was in the middle of nowhere. The person could have shot him or knocked him unconscious and taken anything they wanted without going through all this. It really didn't add up. He couldn't come up with one single reason why someone would kidnap him. The only logical conclusion was the illogical. It had to be some kind of maniac about to do God only knows what to him, before disposing of his mutilated body.

From out of the blue, he felt a tingle start up in his limbs. It was the feeling you get when you've sat on the toilet for too long and your legs have fallen asleep, then you stand up. The moan that issued from his throat was involuntary, but welcome all the same. It was the first sound he'd been able to make.

Straining with all his might, he was able to twitch his hands and feet. Then, all at once, he was able to move about freely as if nothing had been wrong in the first place. But he noticed something important had occurred during his reintroduction to movement; the car had stopped, and the engine had been turned off.

He cocked his head in an effort to hear what was going on. Everything was silent. He placed his ear next to the trunk's seal, but no sound filtered through. Trevor had just contorted his 6' 3", 170-pound, thin body into a position to kick in the backseat, when a metallic clinking gave him pause.

His hand reached down and traced the tools, or in this case, weapons that he used when he was called to fix something at a client's house. In his haste to escape, he had forgotten all about them. Trevor might not be in the best shape of his life, but with a chisel, hammer, or screwdriver, he was strong enough to do some real damage. Especially if his abductor still thought he was incapacitated.

He felt around until he found one of his medium sized

chisels and carefully placed it in his pocket. Then he slowly dug back into the pile until he found a large, flat-head screwdriver. He cuffed it along his leg and laid back in the position he'd been in when he woke up.

Long minutes passed with no sound reaching his ears. The awkward position was starting to be unbearable. Sweat beaded all over his body. He needed something to happen quick or he'd be forced to move and give away the element of surprise. Footfalls crunching over a rocky surface caused adrenaline to flood his system. A calm voice spoke, letting him know his effort had been for naught.

"You've been able to move for about two minutes now. Just wanted you to know that I have a gun pointed at the center of the trunk. Try anything and I kill you, then go after your two children."

The voice was so matter of fact that Trevor was forced to believe every word. But, as a man, could he just go along with the guy's plan, whatever it was? His inner masculinity was bellowing, "HELL NO!" But the father in him was saying, "For God's sake, don't risk your kids!"

Dropping the screwdriver noisily so the man could hear the clink, he yelled, "Alright! You win! Just tell me what you want me to do." No answer came, but the trunk's lid popped open to reveal a masked man standing about six feet away, gun extended pointing right at his chest.

The figure was menacing in his all-black attire. It looked as if his whole body was encased in armor. But after a second look, it was just a ton of muscle definition under form-fitting clothes.

This man was a warrior. Probably didn't even need the gun. But the accessory made it perfectly clear that he was the one in charge.

In a smooth voice, his captor said, "Get out. If you have anything on you, leave it in the trunk, or I make another stop after this one."

Trevor was scrambling out of the car when he remembered the chisel in his pocket. He settled back down and dropped it next to the rest of the tools. Shrugging, he looked up and said, "Sorry. I forgot I put it there," before climbing out and stretching his cramped legs.

Gazing around, he took in as much of his environment as he could. They were parked on a dirt and rock road that dead-ended at a field. It was bordered by hefty trees and underbrush so thick in places, you'd need a machete to navigate inside. He didn't need any more validation to know exactly where he was, but the moon cast just enough illumination to make him tremble with the realization. They were at the back entrance to the Morganton Memorial Cemetery.

The actual headstones didn't start for a couple hundred yards to the east, but rumor had it that the place they were about to enter probably held more bodies than the official graveyard. At least that had been the gossip of his youth. Seeing it now, in this state of semi-darkness, with a gun pointed at his chest, he had no reason to doubt those old stories.

Turning his attention back to the gunman, Trevor sized him up. The guy was a couple inches shorter than his own 6' 3", but his bearing made him seem more significant. His build reminded him of Michael B. Jordan in that new boxing flick. He didn't know if it was the black clothing melding with the surrounding night, but the man gave off almost supernatural vibes with his presence. The bag strapped to his back, and the freaky looking mask didn't help matters.

The top of the material conformed to the man's skull, broadcasting that he was either bald or had a very low haircut. The eyes, nose, and mouth covering looked to be a tightly woven mesh that hid the features from sight, but obviously didn't inhabit their use. If he popped up in a child's bedroom in the middle of the night, Trevor was sure the kid would wet himself, thinking some supervillain had come to steal him away. Under the circumstances, Trevor was sure the kid would be right.

"Done?" asked the gunman, referencing Trevor's perusal. He nodded, hoping the gun wouldn't discharge and blow him away. "Good," he said. "Now turn around and walk until I tell you to stop." As much as Trevor hated to turn his back to the guy, he thought it best to follow the directives of someone holding him at gunpoint.

They walked over the uneven dirt, rocks, and grass with the moon illuminating their path. Trevor didn't know if the man was doing it to fuck with him or not, but he matched his crunching footsteps with his own. He turned and looked over his shoulder at the man and got a strong warning for it not to happen again.

"The next time you look back at me, I'll blow out both your knees and detach your limbs using a hammer and chisel from your collection. Do I make myself clear?" Trevor nodded and kept walking, feeling his bowels liquify.

Five more minutes of walking brought them to the very edge of the cemetery's perimeter. A glance to the right unveiled a sight that almost tipped Trevor over the edge into madness. Without conscious thought, he stopped walking. His kidnapper said, "You see it. Head that way or I kill you now." Feeling the first tear roll down his face, he forced his legs to continue their forward motion.

By the time he was told to stop, Trevor was a trembling, whimpering mass of cowardice. There was no other sight in the world that could have broken him to this extent. His eyes searched for anything that could help him escaped this fate, and he found it leaning against a low wall about eight feet away.

The shovel and pickax looked brand new. They were formidable and expensive, a brand that was known to be durable and trustworthy. He knew exactly why the tools were there, he just hoped he could forestall what they were intended for. Maybe get the chance to use them for his own purposes. He would have to continue acting defeated until the man got complacent, then he could capitalize on the fatal mistake.

As if Trevor didn't know what to do, the man said, "I already marked the area. Use the shovel and pickax to dig the rest of the way. Before you start, turn around and look at me."

Trevor turned and the man said, "You will have a chance to live, but first, you'll have to master your fears to keep your life. Don't do anything foolish that will force me to remove that chance."

Trevor, having gathered himself enough to calm down, asked, "Why? Why are you doing this?"

His captor walked over to the edge of the woods and turned holding a foldable lawn chair. He came back and sat it down about 20 feet from where Trevor would be digging. After stripping the bag off and sitting with a relieved sigh, he said, "All will be disclosed in due time. Now, start digging." Trevor stared for a few seconds, then walked over to the tools and got to work. He would get his chance, he just hoped he would have enough energy left to carry it out.

The rocky soil was hard to move, but that wasn't the only thing he was struggling with. He was battling hysteria with every shovel full of dirt he threw. His knees were weak with misery because his worst nightmare was about to come true. This couldn't be a coincidence. Somehow, someway, this guy had found out what happened to him almost 40 years ago.

It had been a night not unlike the one he was enduring now. He and a group of boys had decided to try and scare each other with ghost stories. Being young and dumb led to this very area of the cemetery that housed some of the oldest graves. Unbeknownst to him, two of the older boys had set up a trap for their own amusement.

One of their favorite ways to test each other was playing truth or dare. When it was his turn, one of the boys dared him to jump from grave to grave along the back row of the cemetery. He balked, but the ragging got so bad, he finally gave into the pressure.

He bounced from one grave to the next, feeling more confident as he passed each one. Then the trap was sprung. The boys had dug up one of the graves and placed a mat of grass above the opening. When he fell in, his ankle snapped and he screamed in agony. But the other kids thought he was faking the injury.

They laughed gleefully and called him every derogatory name in the book. Being that he was the only black kid in the group, the name calling took a very ugly turn. His tears of pain and embarrassment had little effect on their enjoyment. As they continued to laugh, they all grabbed shovels and started tossing dirt in on top of him.

It wasn't too bad, the shovelfuls of dirt couldn't bury him, but then another group of kids showed up.

Markedly older, once they found out what was going on, one of them ran over to the toolshed and grabbed the keys to the front loader. When Trevor heard the engine spring to life, he knew that the boys truly meant to kill him.

Within seconds, he heard the wheels churning towards his location. He tried to climb the sides as the excited snickers of the kids blended with his own shouts of alarm. The driver yelled for him to say a prayer, then dumped the load directly over his head. Maybe he would have been fine had the mix not contained the small boulder.

The stone struck him and he fell flat on his back. The next thing he knew, he was completely submerged under the unyielding weight of the dirt.

It felt like he suffocated for hours. He would lose consciousness just to regain it moments later to suffer a little more before going out again. When he woke the next day in the hospital, his so-called friends told him he'd only been under for about 45 seconds before they pulled him out. But the panic he felt, as the weight pressed the air from his lungs, made him claustrophobic for the rest of his life. Realizing that he might have to relive that experience again really soon, he was desperate to find some way to change his future.

Hours passed as he continued to dig. The night was not hot at all, but the chilled air did little to wick the sweat from his body. The hole was now deeper than his waist. His energy was waning fast, he had to figure some kind of way to get his captor close enough for him to have his shot.

"Hey man!" he yelled to get his attention. "How deep do

you want this thing?"

The man jolted as if he'd been sleeping, and Trevor silently kicked himself for not trying something else before alerting him. He stood up, stretched as if he'd been the one laboring all fucking night, and walked over to the side of the hole.

He said, "Maybe a couple more feet and you'll be finished." When he turned to walk away, Trevor took advantage of the brief opportunity.

He swung the shovel at his legs with every bit of power he could muster. Trevor didn't make a sound, and he made absolutely sure the man turned fully before his attempt. But the bastard must have eyes in the back of his head. With a small shuffle step, Trevor watched with dismay as the shovel breezed by the intended target, harmlessly. With little fanfare, the guy turned around, pulled out his gun, aimed it at his chest, and pulled the trigger.

For a few seconds, Trevor felt like he was floating. All the physical stimuli that told a person they were alive, fled his body.

He couldn't move. The position he landed in provided him a close-up view of a small, neat hole in his t-shirt, directly over his heart. But there was no blood. He tried to raise his hand to assess the damage, but just like in the trunk, his body was frozen.

Rolling his eyes upward, he watched the man as he peeled the mask from his face. Nodding, he said, "I don't blame you for the attempt, a man has to take his shot when the opportunity presents itself. But it's time for the final act. Because of your crimes against helpless inmates, you will be put in the same position they were in. Whether you live or die will be up to your fortitude and fate. My willingness to show my face should tell you which outcome my money's on." With that, he hopped down and tossed Trevor out of the hole with remarkable ease, stretching his body out beside the grave.

With his breath erratic, heartbeat thumping, Trevor watched out the corner of his eye as the man made his way over to the pack sitting next to the chair. Grabbing it, he turned and headed back over to him. As he watched him unpack the bag, Trevor became increasingly confused, until the man started telling him exactly what was going on.

The bald, brown-skinned man said, "I've done my research on you. I know what happened to you as a kid. I also know what got you fired from Foothills Youth Institution. After all the bullshit you went through as a child, why would you turn around and do that to those inmates?" He glanced over with his dark-brown eyes like he expected a reply. Obviously, Trevor was in no condition to answer.

He continued. "The fact that you only targeted the black kids speaks to how much you really abhor yourself. And I bet you felt justified because they cursed you, or called you a name. Instead of being a man and a professional and ignore them, or offer them some help, you chose to torture and persecute them by denying them food. Well, I brought along a few instruments to help you experience a taste, or lack thereof, of what you gave them."

The pack was big enough to fit dozens of items inside. From what Trevor could see, only three were removed. His captor picked up the first of them and explained its use while putting it on Trevor's body.

"I know you're probably thinking, 'Why the hell do I need a lifejacket on dry land?' Well, this one has been modified to fulfill my objective. The weight of the dirt, as you know, can crush you and leave you unconscious in seconds." Pressing something on the side of the jacket, it inflated to twice the capacity of a normal one. "This will provide a little relief so your lungs can function. I want you to live as long as possible, suffering until you draw your last, agonized breath."

Next, he picked up the mask that made him think about Star Wars for some reason. He placed it on Trevor's face, completely covering his nose, ears, eyes, and mouth. "This will make sure you have plenty of air. So, when you draw in those deep breaths, that oxygen will guarantee your muscles feel the maximum level of pain. You'll understand as you get closer to the end." He smiled and winked as if they were two friends sharing an intimate joke.

He made sure the breathing apparatus fit nice and snug on his face, secured the strap around his head so it wouldn't move, then reached for the last item. Even before he started to hook it to the mask, the ten-foot length of hose was pretty self-explanatory. Now, Trevor was able to get a clear picture of what was about to happen to him. But his captor still took the time to explain the purpose of the hose.

"So, this little bit of clear plastic and rubber will be the only thing keeping you alive. At the beginning, you will feel blessed to have it. By the end, you will be cursing its very existence."

He bent over and attached one end to a port on the side of the mask. "It's long enough for you to move it around in case it rains or becomes clogged with dirt. I'll leave some of it in your hand so you have a little play if something happens." Then he reached in his pocket, pulled out a pair of tweezers, and removed a small mass from the hole in

Trevor's shirt.

"About 30 minutes from now, you'll have your full range of motion back." Shrugging, he added, "Won't matter that much, you'll be under a ton of dirt restricting that movement."

The man was efficient, Trevor had to give him that. Within seconds, he had him laid out in the four-foot hole, flat on his back, the other end of the air hose hooked to something above ground, keeping it out of the way.

The first scrape of the shovel, as it dug into the pile of loose dirt, caused Trevor to lose his mind for a while. His torturous screams echoed around in his head, only because he had lost the ability to release them. If he was able to force the bloodcurdling sounds out into the chilled, night air, he would probably have corpses rising out of their graves to investigate the hellacious noise. Maybe they would help him. Maybe he'd become a late-night snack. Whatever happened had to be better than the punishment he was about to endure.

The first grains of dirt striking his face brought him back to reality. His eyes widened when he glimpsed nothing but dirt below his neck. Those muscles were not just for show. This guy was like a machine, he thought, as scoop after scoop continued to engulf his body. Only a couple minutes passed before he could no longer see nor feel the dirt encasing him in his tomb.

But he could hear the creatures. He could hear the crawly things making their way, shifting and sliding closer to the fleshy meal they had just been served. They were rushing to be the first ones to sample a treat they were normally denied: warm blooded meat, still tender and juicy and fresh.

After listening for a few minutes, he cursed his

overactive imagination. He realized what he was hearing was the scrape and rasp of the shovel through the air hose.

His laugh startled him for a second, he hadn't realized he was free from his invisible constraints. But then he found himself truly afraid, the mountain of dirt really did hold him immobile. No amount of twisting or turning gained him an inch of mobility. He blinked a couple times behind the mask and thanked God for small favors. If he would've been forced to keep his eyes closed, he would have gone crazy in minutes, even though with them open, he still couldn't see shit.

Speaking of his mind, he needed to focus on how to get out of here. He could still hear the shoveler performing his demonic task, but that only told him that all the dirt wasn't in place yet. Which meant this was the time to do something, while the dirt was still loose and hadn't had time to settle.

He worked his head from side to side, front to back, up and down. He wasn't imagining it! The dirt was shifting and compacting, giving his head more room to maneuver. He tried the same thing with his hands, finding that the fresh dirt wasn't hard to move at all, you just had to do it little by little. His heart flooded with hope as he went about the task, abruptly stopping when a new sound assaulted his ears.

Voices! Definitely more than one. He screamed, "HELP! Help me! I'm down here!" in an effort to signal the newcomer to the atrocity being committed. After screaming until his throat started to burn, he shut his mouth and listened to the conversation taking place over his body. He needed all the info he could get if he planned on getting out of this alive.

The man holding the shovel looked across the freshly covered grave and tried to decide if he needed to dig another one. The second hole wouldn't need to be as deep because the body in it would be beyond saving. As if the newcomer could read his thoughts, he kept his hands up in a sign of peace, a smile plastered across his face.

"What the fuck are you doing here?" the kidnapper demanded, eyeing the newcomer up and down. His eyes also tracking around to make sure the man was alone.

The Burberry, wool and cashmere, sweater, paired with the Canali trousers, cost somewhere in the ballpark of $2,000. Add in the Brioni overcoat, and the Kemo Sabe, suede boots, and the idiot was in a cemetery, in the middle of the night, wearing a $13,000 outfit. He didn't seem to mind though; money was of little consequence to those who had tons of it.

The slim white man spread his arms farther apart and said, "I just came to see if you were okay. You didn't leave our last meeting with the best disposition."

Before he could respond to the comment, former Officer Trevor Jones decided to intrude on their little get together. They stood staring at each other as the buried man yelled for help from what he thought could be his savior. What he didn't know is he was a lot safer in the hands of the captor than in the devious hands of the newcomer.

Not wanting to waste any more time, the shovel holder talked over the muted screams. "Cut the bullshit and tell me why you're here! Who sent you?"

In his soft, calm voice, the newcomer said, "I swear, no one sent me. I was just doing a random check and came to make sure you were good." After a long pause, he pointed at the grave and asked, "And who might this be?"

"Personal," was the only answer he gave.

"So, nothing dealing with us?" asked the older white man.

"Look," he said, dropping the shovel. "I got this. I know what I'm doing. Just stay the fuck out of my way and I might see you at the end of all this."

The newcomer was smart and knew when he had overstayed his welcome. Taking a few steps back, he said, "Just want you to know you're on your own in this. No one will aid you, but some will want to stop you. My advice, you're making a huge mistake and it's gonna get you killed. Let the past be the past and let this silly mission die. Nothing good can come of it."

Having heard enough, the man pulled his gun and pointed it at the newcomer. "Fuck you and your advice. But while we're advising, let me give you some for the road. I'm gonna complete my mission, and anyone who gets in my way will die. The number of bodies hasn't been etched in stone, but I can guarantee that mine won't be added to it. Stay the fuck out of my way and let me teach you how to do what needs to be done. My revenge is certain. You just need to decide if you want to be part of the solution, or part of the problem."

The newcomer took several more steps back, still keeping his hands in plain view. "Have it your way. I'm neutral in this. You can have your hunt for vengeance, but I want you to be absolutely sure you're willing to pay the price to achieve that goal."

"The price has already been paid. I earned this right, and you can bet your last dollar that I'm gonna see it through."

Pointing the gun at the other man's head, he said, "This is the only pass you get. The next time you interfere, you die. Now go, before I change my mind."

Again, the newcomer was very smart. He knew when he had overstayed his welcome. This time, he turned without a word and drifted off into the night.

The shoveler finished up the hole by laying a patch of fake grass over it and picking up the air hose. So Trevor could hear him, he said, "This is karma coming to collect the debt that you owe. All those people, children, that you decided were worthless and weak, now they have someone to avenge them. I've been planning this for a long time, and though you don't know me, I'm a strategist on a level you can't even fathom.

"I'm giving you a chance to live," he continued. "And if you do, you'll have survived your sentence and I'll leave you be. But this is only the beginning. If you submit to death, know that you won't be lonely for long. I can't say that I'm a messenger from God, but my message will surely touch a lot of souls. Any questions before I leave?"

A few whimpers and deep breaths echoed down the hose before a small, deflated voice asked, "Who are you?"

A cloud passed across the face of the moon, casting the entire area into darkness. He thought the atmosphere was fitting to deliver his final message. "I am the force that will bring vengeance to the powerful who practice their sinful ways unchecked. The man who will wage war to collect the debt the guilty ones owe. I am the cold hand of death that everyone in my path will feel and shiver. I am the price of doing evil. I am RETRIBUTION!"

With that, he dropped the hose and gathered all evidence

that the area had recently been in use. Returning to the Honda Accord, it didn't take him long to deliver it back to the driveway of the soon to be dead Trevor Jones.

From there, he walked the half mile to the abandoned farmhouse where he had stashed his own vehicle. His night was finished, but his mission was just getting started. He'd made his statement to one group, now it was time for the other side to hear his message. Turning the key, he steered the car to the road and made a left, heading east towards Elizabeth City, where his next target awaited his fate.

4 DAYS LATER

The night was pitch-black with a brisk, chilled wind whipping through the congested trees. The children stepped out of the woods and glanced around nervously, not knowing what to expect. Their parents had always warned them to stay out of this area. But telling a child to stay away just made the place that much more desirable.

The biggest kid looked at the others and snickered. "You hear that noise? That's the sound ghouls make when they smell a fresh, tasty meal."

A slightly smaller boy, bundled up against the cool temperature, said, "Shut up, Vinni! If that's true, you're the one that should be worried." Fanning his nose, he said, "I'm sure they could smell you from a mile away." The other two kids giggled as Vinni punched the boy's arm in retaliation.

"Keep it up, smart ass," said Vinni. "I wanna see some of that same spunk when it's your turn to go."

The four 12-year-old boys had been best friends since they could remember. From preschool all the way up to the present, they'd been inseparable. And the dynamics had been the same from the beginning: Vinni and Mike vied to see who was more dominant, while Kevin and Jesse watched with barely contained anticipation.

The two leaders could and would fight over anything. It was a toss-up who would win from day to day. But one thing you could hang your hat on, if anyone else challenged any member of their group, the two would combine forces and destroy all adversaries.

Tonight was the night they'd been waiting for all month. Their parents had gone to some fancy fundraiser in Shelby,

North Carolina, and were staying overnight. Since Vinni's house was the biggest, they had convinced their parents to let them all stay there together so they would only need to hire one sitter. His house was also the closest to the graveyard, so all the boys rejoiced when they were given the okay.

The girl their parents hired was a hot, 17-year-old blond who had sat for all of them at one time or another over the years. She loved to boss them around and threaten them with an early bedtime. But she could be bought.

The boys had pooled their money and came up with a grand total of $24.15. She said that such a small sum would only buy them two and a half hours of freedom, and not a second longer. They had whooped and hollered, bundled up to combat the windy night, then ran full out the whole trip through the woods. They didn't want to waste a second that could be spent playing The Game.

Like most young boys, they enjoyed playing video games and competing in sports. They liked riding bikes and spying on the neighborhood girls when they felt they could get away with it. But nothing could hold their attention like The Game.

It started as most things do for kids, when they had been 2nd graders, they'd come across a group of 5th graders playing The Game. Others called it Truth or Dare, but to them, it was something greater than just a truth or a dare. It was a way to prove your manhood. Nothing you could ever do on X-Box or on a basketball court could ever top completing a dare that others were too afraid to do. Hence, The Game was born.

As they turned in unison, heading deeper into the clearing, Vinni kept up the talk, trying his best to sike everyone out. "My dad told me that over a hundred kids have gone missing in this graveyard. The ones they do find are so full of terror, they come back mute and can only sleep with the lights on."

Mike said, "Yeah, it makes sense that your dad would know. He probably has most of them still chained up in your basement." Vinni took another swipe at him as Kevin and Jesse cracked up.

"Mike, you're really asking for it!" proclaimed Vinni. "My dad can kick your dad's ass any day of the week!"

"Your dad's a fantasy writer, Vinni. My dad works at the prison. The Maximum-Security Prison!" Mike boasted proudly. "While your dad is making up villains, my dad kicks villain ass all day. Maybe in that stupid book you're always writing your dad could win, but not in the real world."

This time, Kevin and Jesse remained quiet as they walked along behind the dueling pair. Vinni hated when anyone downed his book. Most of the fights the two had, came after one of Mike's hurled insults about Vinni's work.

As expected, Vinni said, "My book isn't stupid! When I've sold a Trillion copies and I go down in history as the greatest writer of all times, then what will you say?"

"I'll say, I know the guy who sold a Trillion copies of the stupidest book ever written!" said Mike before he took off running, Vinni hot on his heels.

Mike was fast. By far the fastest of the four boys. Knowing that Vinni didn't have a chance in hell of catching him, from time to time, Mike would turn and run backwards, taunting the bigger boy. Kevin and Jesse, not wanting to be left alone out there in the darkness, ran after the pair, yelling for them to stop fighting. They were just getting tired of running when Mike tripped over something laying in the grass, taking a hard fall as a result. Vinni, having reached his boiling point, dove on Mike and the fighting ensued.

Since Vinni was huffing and puffing from the long, drawn-out run, this wasn't much of a fight, at least not compared to some of their other battles. Within seconds, Mike was straddling Vinni's back, spanking his ass, pretending to ride his prone body like a horse. After he rolled off, even Vinni couldn't help but join in the raucous laughter of his friends.

After a few minutes, the boys regained their purpose and formed the circle that signified the beginning of The Game. Kevin, with his shoulder-length dreadlocks, was the first to notice it. "What's that?" he asked, pointing at the ground.

They all looked down and Mike said, "I think that's what I tripped over." Giving it a good kick, he said, "Probably some tool the junkies use to do their drugs, fucking losers! Now, are we playing The Game, or not? We need to stay focused!"

Kevin, leaning over farther, said, "Wait a minute! I think this thing is going underground!" He picked up the end and tracked the hose to a small hole about three feet away. Looking up, he whispered, "One of the missing kids could be under there!"

Vinni hacked out a laugh. "Stop being such a little baby. They're just ghost stories! You really believe kids go missing here? Name me one kid from our school who has gone missing!" challenged Vinni.

Jesse, the smartest one in the group, said, "Statistics show that a child is kidnapped in America every few minutes. Maybe this is just one of the hiding places for kidnappers from out of town." No one commented because Jesse was rarely wrong when it came to these types of things.

Mike wouldn't pass up an opportunity like this for a Million bucks. "Alright, Mr. High And Mighty, I dare you to communicate with the kid buried under the dirt!"

Thinking this was the easiest dare Mike had ever given him, Vinni reached out and snatched the hose from Kevin's hand. "That's the best you could come up with? We're in a cemetery and the best dare you have is for me to speak to some imaginary kid?" Laughing, he brought the end up to his mouth and said, "Hey, Missing Kid! You want to tell me who kidnapped and buried you?"

Everyone was laughing and teasing Mike for giving such an easy dare, until Vinni stopped and dropped the hose, taking a step back. The boys all went quiet when they saw the look on his face. Mike glanced at the tube and asked, "Something wrong?"

Vinni took a couple more steps back and said, "The hose moved in my hand." Looking up at Mike, he said, "Someone pulled it or something." None of the boys could tell if he was being serious or if this was just more mind games.

Kevin and Jesse glanced at each other, both backing away from the hose. Kevin said, "Stop being a jerk, Vinni! You're just making that up to try and scare us!" From the quake in his voice, he'd passed scared a long time ago.

Shaking his head, Vinni said, "I swear man! Someone's down there!"

Smirking, not fooled for a second by the scared act, Mike said, "Yeah right! If someone's down there, why isn't it moving now?" As if he'd spoken it into existence, they all screamed when the plastic tube wiggled right in their faces.

Kevin, Jesse, and Vinni took off running, screaming from the shock. Mike wanted to run, but he stood, petrified in place, staring down at the clear tube. He finally looked up when it registered that all three of his friends were yelling for him to flee. But he couldn't leave. Not without being one hundred percent sure that they weren't imagining this whole thing. With no thought for his own safety, he reached down and snagged the hose, not willing to be a chicken along with his buddies.

With his eyes on his friends as they waited at the tree line, he shakily brought the opening up to his mouth. "Hello?" he whispered. "Is anyone there?"

Quickly, he moved the end to his ear to listen to the response, if it came. He heard nothing. Feeling like a doofus, he brought it up to his mouth once more. Louder this time, he said, "If you're down there, kid, you better say something now, or I'm out of here!"

He was fully convinced that the wind had moved the tube while it had been laying on the ground. Sticking it in his ear once again, he expected to hear the same thing he heard the last time, silence. That's why no one could blame him for pissing his pants after hearing the urgent, "HELP ME! PLEASE, HELP ME!"

But Mike didn't help him. In fact, Mike proved just how fast he truly was as he beat his friends back to the house by a couple of minutes. His friends peppered him with questions, but Mike never spoke on what he'd heard. The only thing he demanded was that they keep all the lights on until he could make it back to his own home.

Had any of the boys stayed to help, it wouldn't have done much good. After another desperate, whispered plea for help, former Officer Trevor Jones took his last breath and succumbed to his torturous sentence. The first victim, spearheading the hoard that would soon follow him into the depths of hell.

ABOUT THE AUTHOR

Leon A. Burch was born in Philadelphia, PA and now resides in North Carolina. He attended Temple University. L. A. Burch started writing in 2022. His first book was released in 2024 and two more have been released since then.

To contact L.A. Burch with questions or comments please feel free to reach out to him at authorlaburch@gmail.com.